MALCOLM'S MARTIANS: EXPLORING MARS

The Meteor Shower: Seeking Shelter

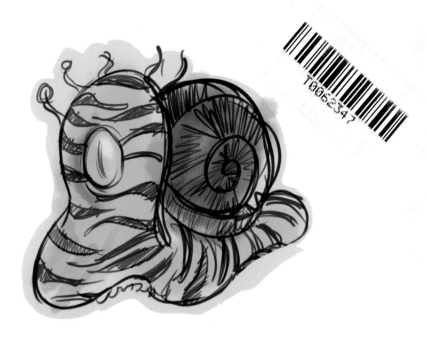

by Jason M. Burns

illustrated by Dustin Evans

TORCH GRAPHIC PRESS

Published in the United States of America by Cherry Lake Publishing Group
Ann Arbor, Michigan
www.cherrylakepublishing.com

Reading Adviser: Beth Walker Gambro, MS, Ed., Reading Consultant, Yorkville, IL

Book Designer: Book Buddy Media

Torch Graphic Press is an imprint of Cherry Lake Publishing Group.

Library of Congress Cataloging-in-Publication Data has been filed and is available at catalog.loc.gov

Cherry Lake Publishing Group would like to acknowledge the work of the Partnership for 21st Century Learning, a Network of Battelle for Kids. Please visit http://www.battelleforkids.org/networks/p21 for more information.

Printed in the United States of America
Corporate Graphics

TABLE OF CONTENTS

Mission log: July 30, 2055.

Today we are visiting the plains. I didn't even know Mars had plains! If there were Martians, I bet they would be herd animals like buffalo and horses. I'm sure my friend Daniela will have some good advice on why they like to live in groups like that. Dad keeps talking about all of the "cereal bowls" out in the plains. I can't wait to see what he is talking about. It's going to be another great adventure!

—Malcolm Thomas

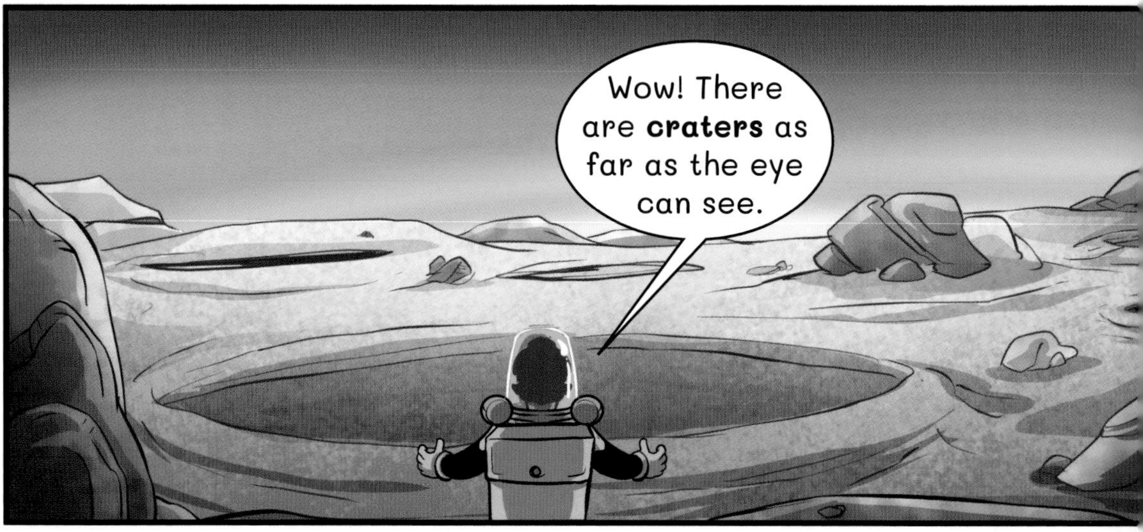
Wow! There are **craters** as far as the eye can see.

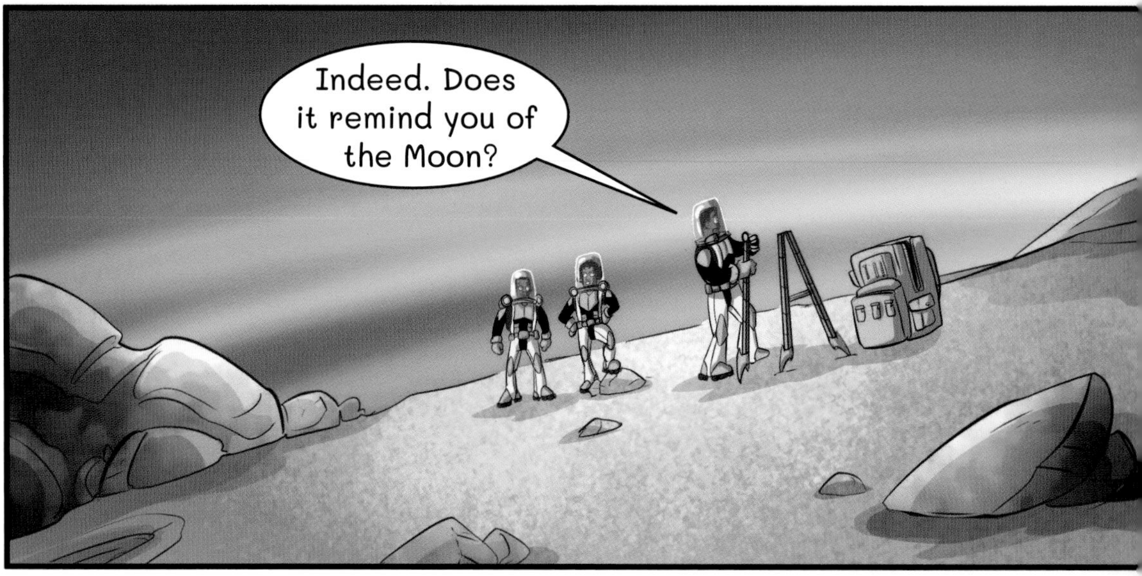
Indeed. Does it remind you of the Moon?

SCIENCE FACT

Earth does not have many craters. They get filled in with dirt and rocks. Wind wears down the sides. The Moon and Mars are full of craters because there is nothing to alter the landscape and fill them in.

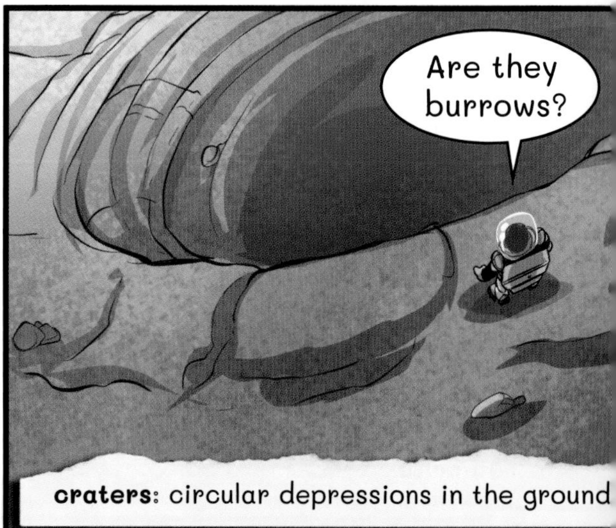
Are they burrows?

craters: circular depressions in the ground

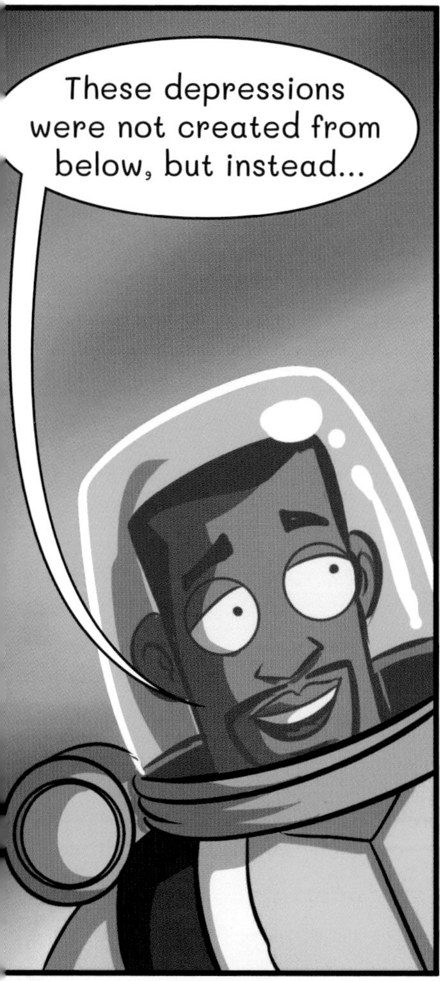
These depressions were not created from below, but instead...

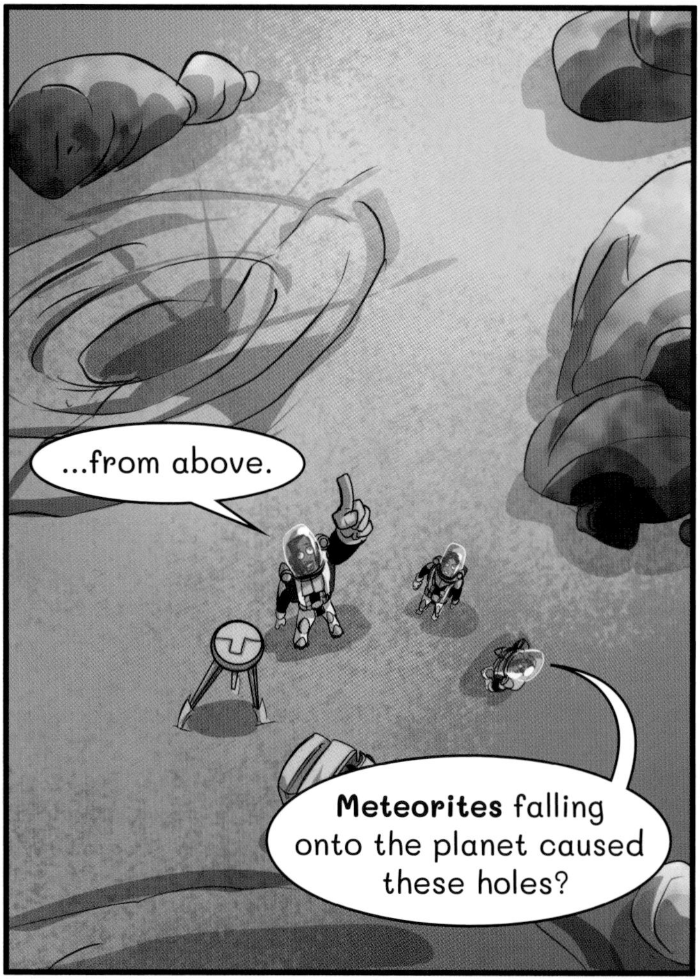
...from above.
Meteorites falling onto the planet caused these holes?

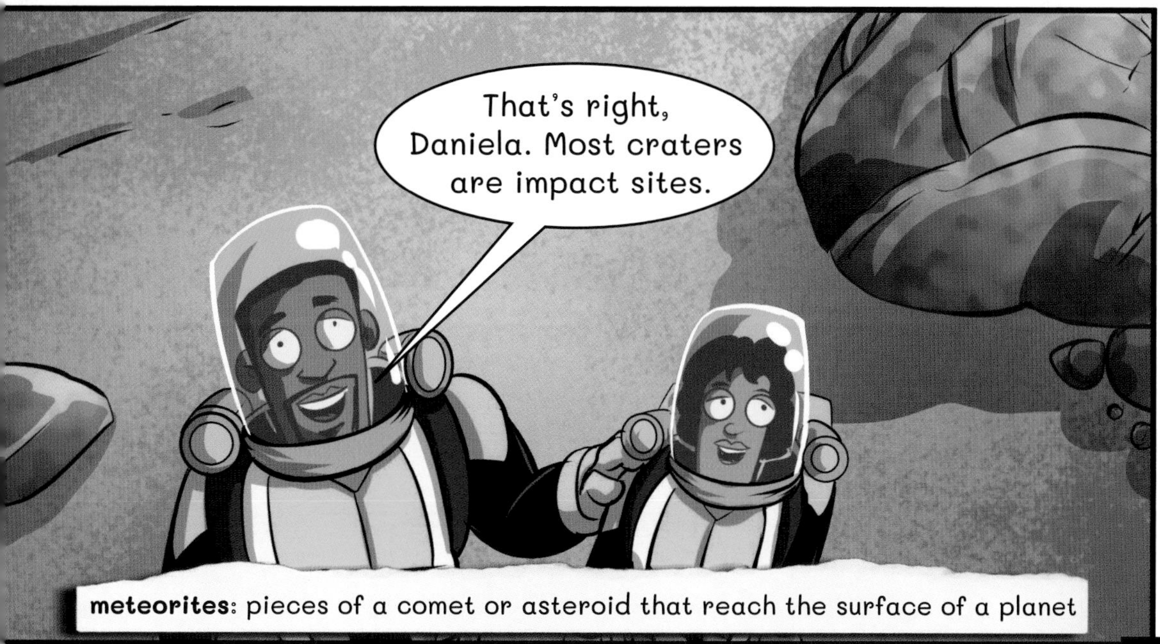
That's right, Daniela. Most craters are impact sites.

meteorites: pieces of a comet or asteroid that reach the surface of a planet

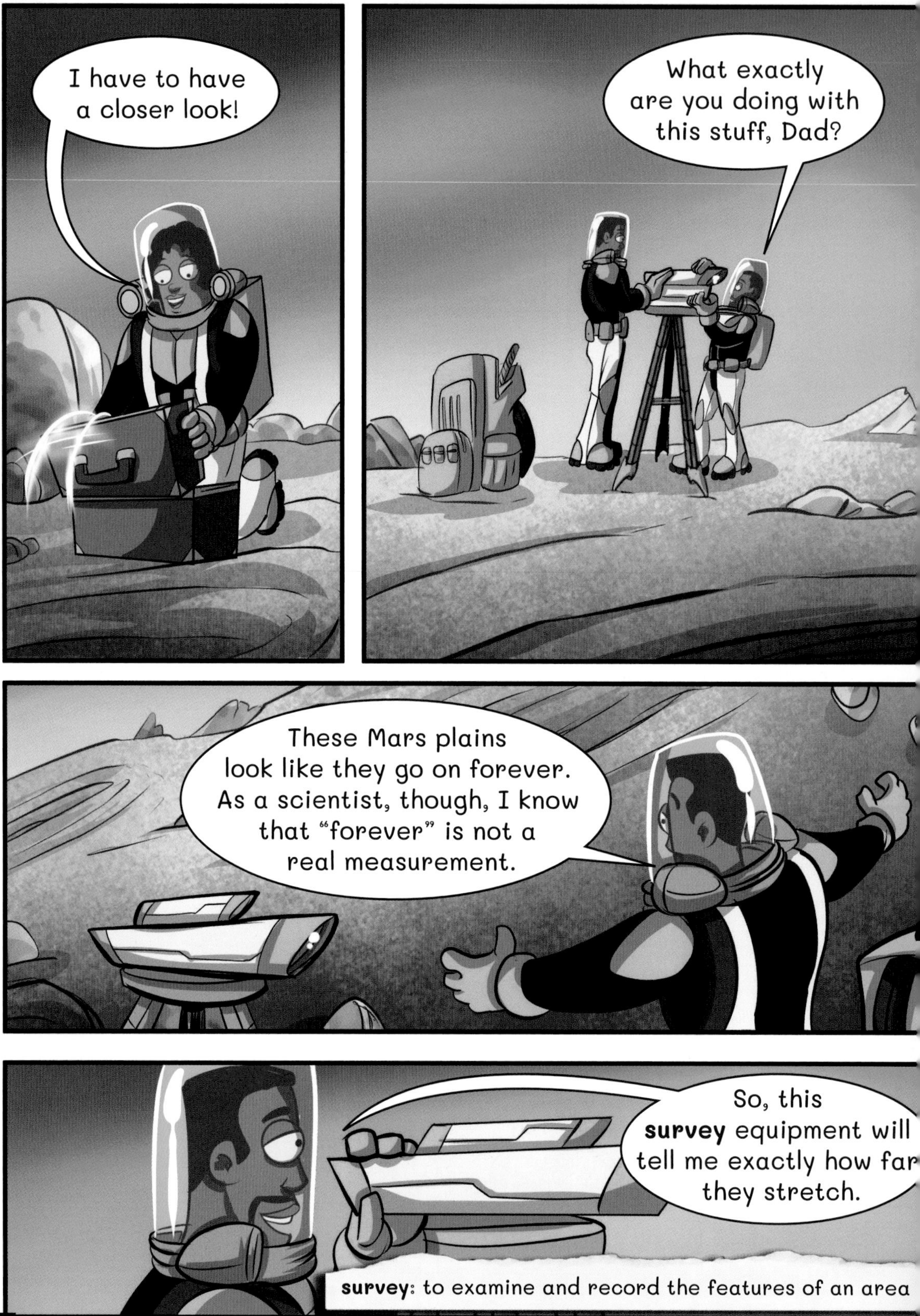
I have to have a closer look!
What exactly are you doing with this stuff, Dad?
These Mars plains look like they go on forever. As a scientist, though, I know that "forever" is not a real measurement.
So, this **survey** equipment will tell me exactly how far they stretch.

survey: to examine and record the features of an area

THE CASE FOR SPACE

Earth isn't the only planet to be visited by meteorites. Plenty of these space rocks have hit Mars too. Thanks to science, we know a lot more about the craters and the meteorites that causes them.

- Scientists estimate Mars has more than 43,000 impact craters with diameters greater than 3 miles (5 kilometers).

- By comparison, only about 120 impact craters have been found on Earth.

- The size and depth of an impact crater depends on how big and how fast the meteorite was.

- Craters are shaped like bowls. This is because the meteorite causes an explosion that is evenly distributed.

- Most meteorites are made of rock or metal.

- It is believed that the majority of the impact craters on Mars were formed early in the planet's life cycle.

- Not all of Mars is covered in craters. However, it might have had craters everywhere long ago. Flowing lava and dust storms could have wiped them away.

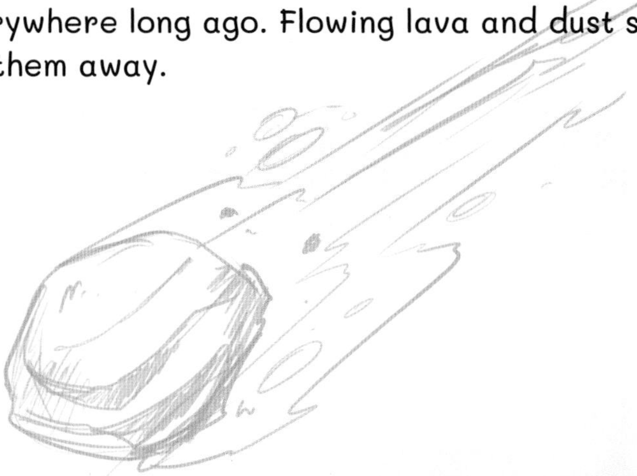

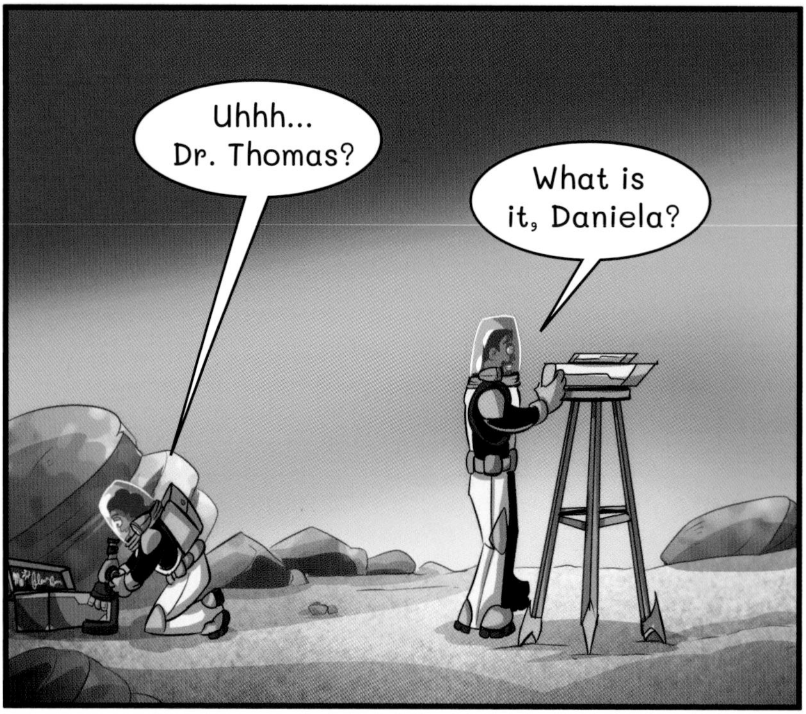
Uhhh...
Dr. Thomas?
What is it, Daniela?

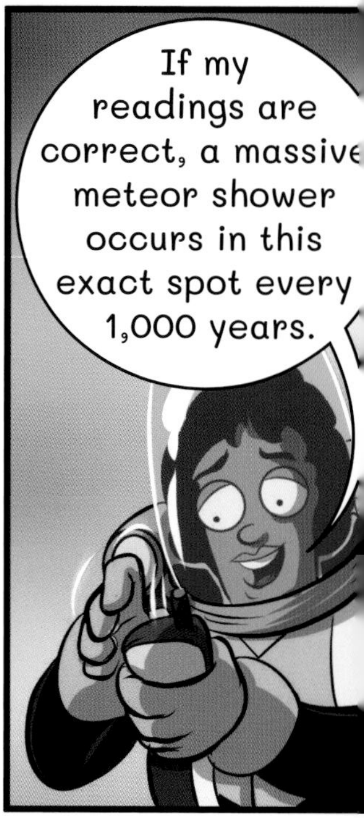
If my readings are correct, a massive meteor shower occurs in this exact spot every 1,000 years.

SCIENCE FACT

Meteor showers are easy to predict. They happen when a planet crosses paths with a **comet**. Comets have set **orbits**, like planets. So they reappear in the same place at sim periods of time.

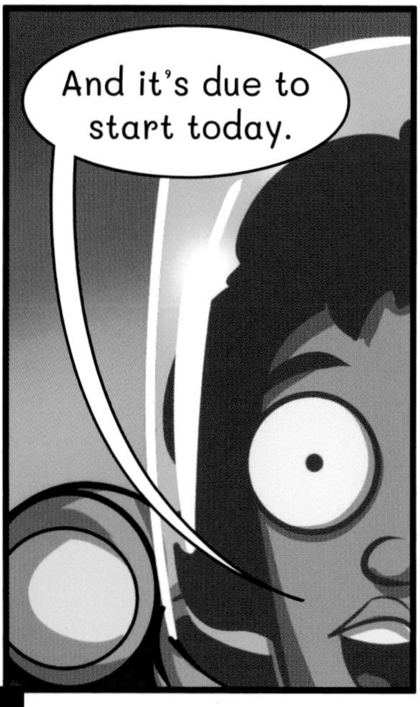
And it's due to start today.

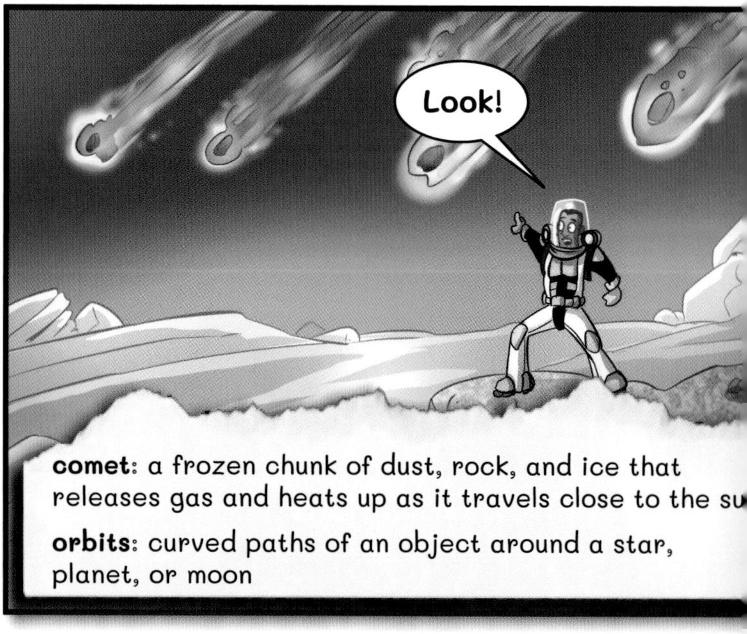
Look!

comet: a frozen chunk of dust, rock, and ice that releases gas and heats up as it travels close to the su

orbits: curved paths of an object around a star, planet, or moon

THE SCIENCE OF SCIENCE FICTION

Researchers can identify new impact craters on Mars using **artificial intelligence**. It may sound like science fiction, but it is all science. Let's take a look at how they do it!

• In the past, researchers identified Mars craters using images captured by Mars orbiters.

• Mars orbiters are robotic spacecraft designed to study the planet from a distance.

• *Mariner 9* became the first spacecraft to orbit Mars in 1971.

• Today, the *Mars Reconnaissance Orbiter* uses a high-resolution camera to take images of the planet. It is so powerful that it can see tracks left by Mars rovers.

• Researchers study these images for changes to the landscape. They use a tool called an **automated** fresh impact crater classifier.

• A series of high-performance computers scan images taken by the orbiters. They detect changes to the landscape. What would take a human researcher 40 minutes now takes just 5 seconds.

• Even though a computer looks at the pictures, a human still needs to check the results. Like a hammer or a screwdriver, the classifier is still only a tool.

artificial intelligence: machines that perform tasks requiring human intelligence

automated: the use of automatic equipment, such as machines

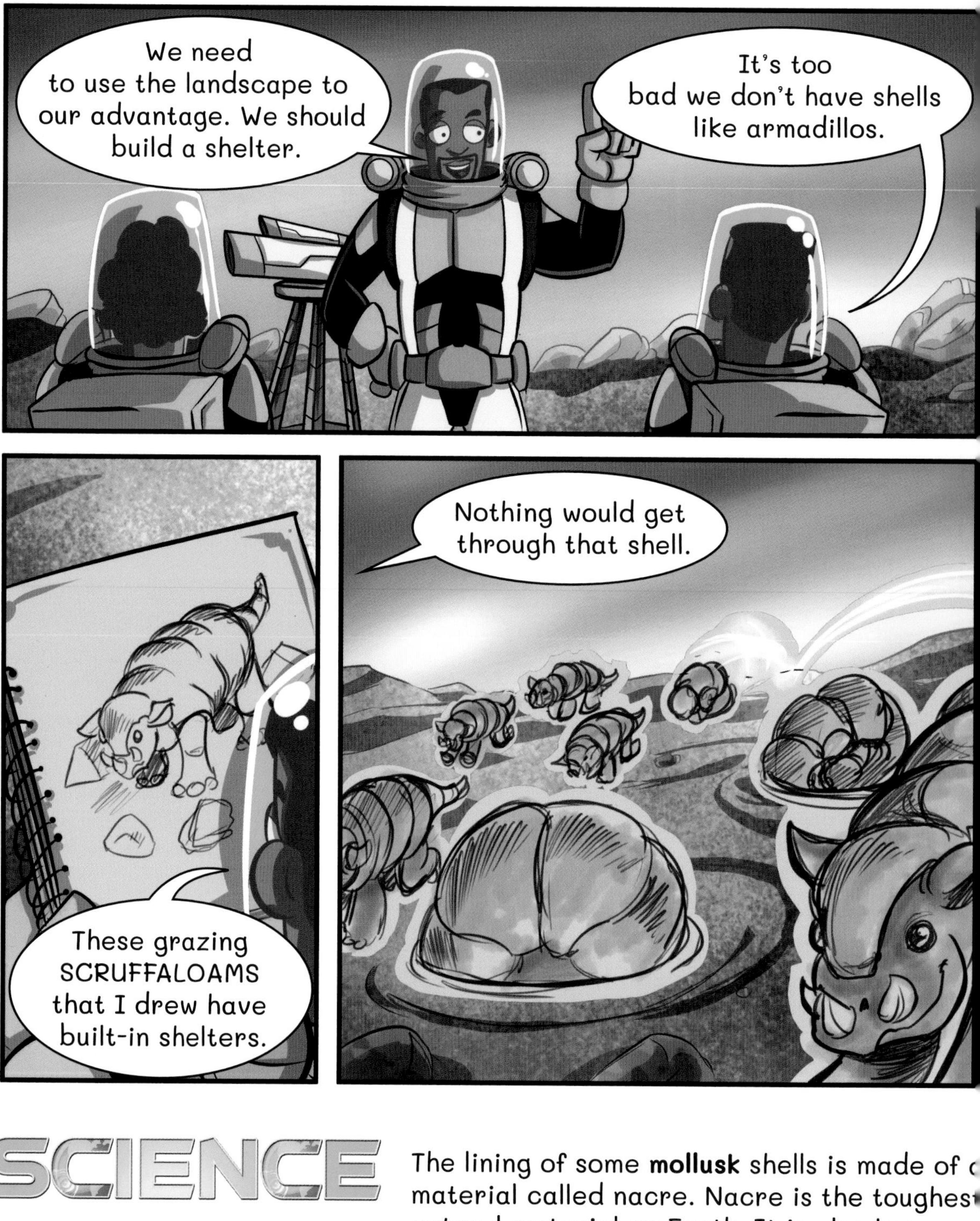
We need to use the landscape to our advantage. We should build a shelter.
It's too bad we don't have shells like armadillos.
These grazing SCRUFFALOAMS that I drew have built-in shelters.
Nothing would get through that shell.

SCIENCE FACT

The lining of some **mollusk** shells is made of material called nacre. Nacre is the toughes natural material on Earth. It is also known as mother-of-pearl.

mollusk: an invertebrate animal, such as snails, mussels, an slugs; mollusks have soft bodies and many have hard shells

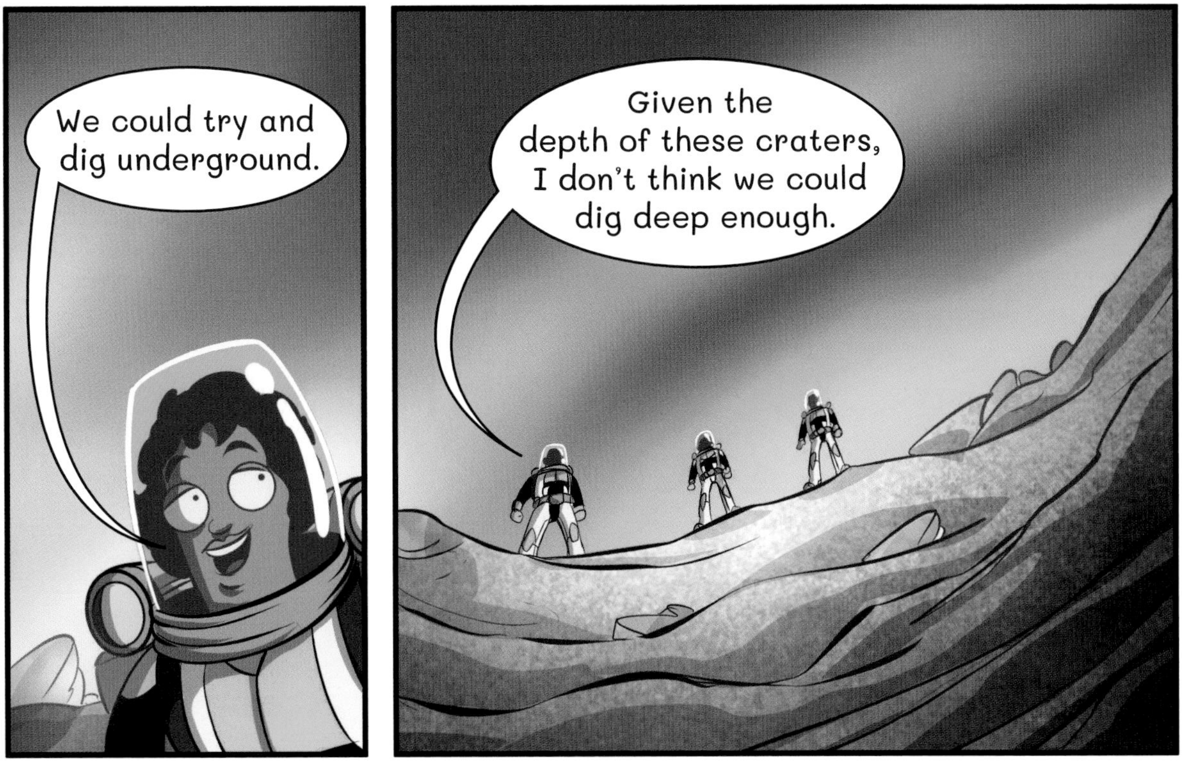
We could try and dig underground.
Given the depth of these craters, I don't think we could dig deep enough.

MARS FACT

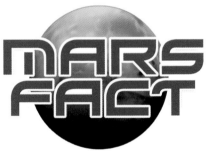

The largest crater discovered on Mars is believed to be twice the size of Alaska. It is called the Hellas basin.

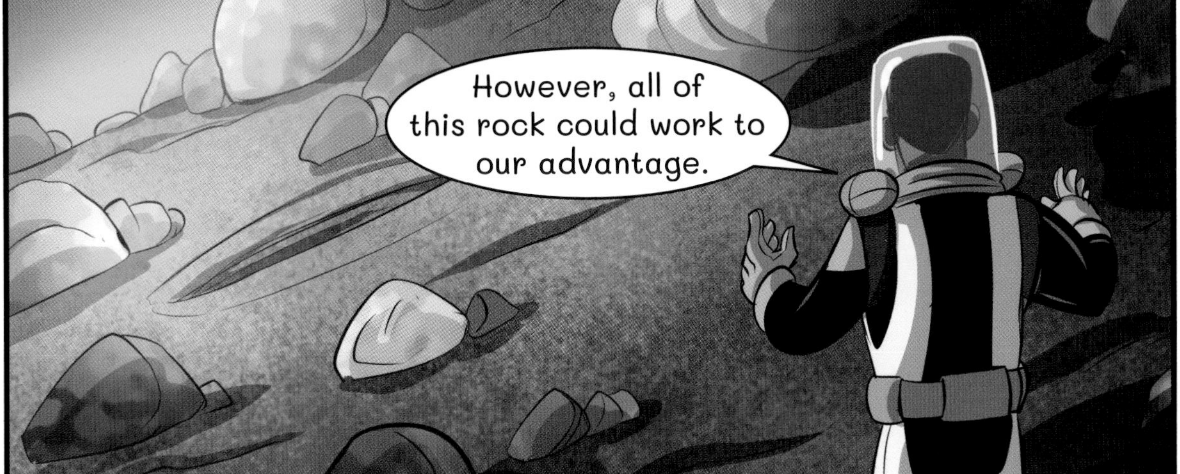
However, all of this rock could work to our advantage.

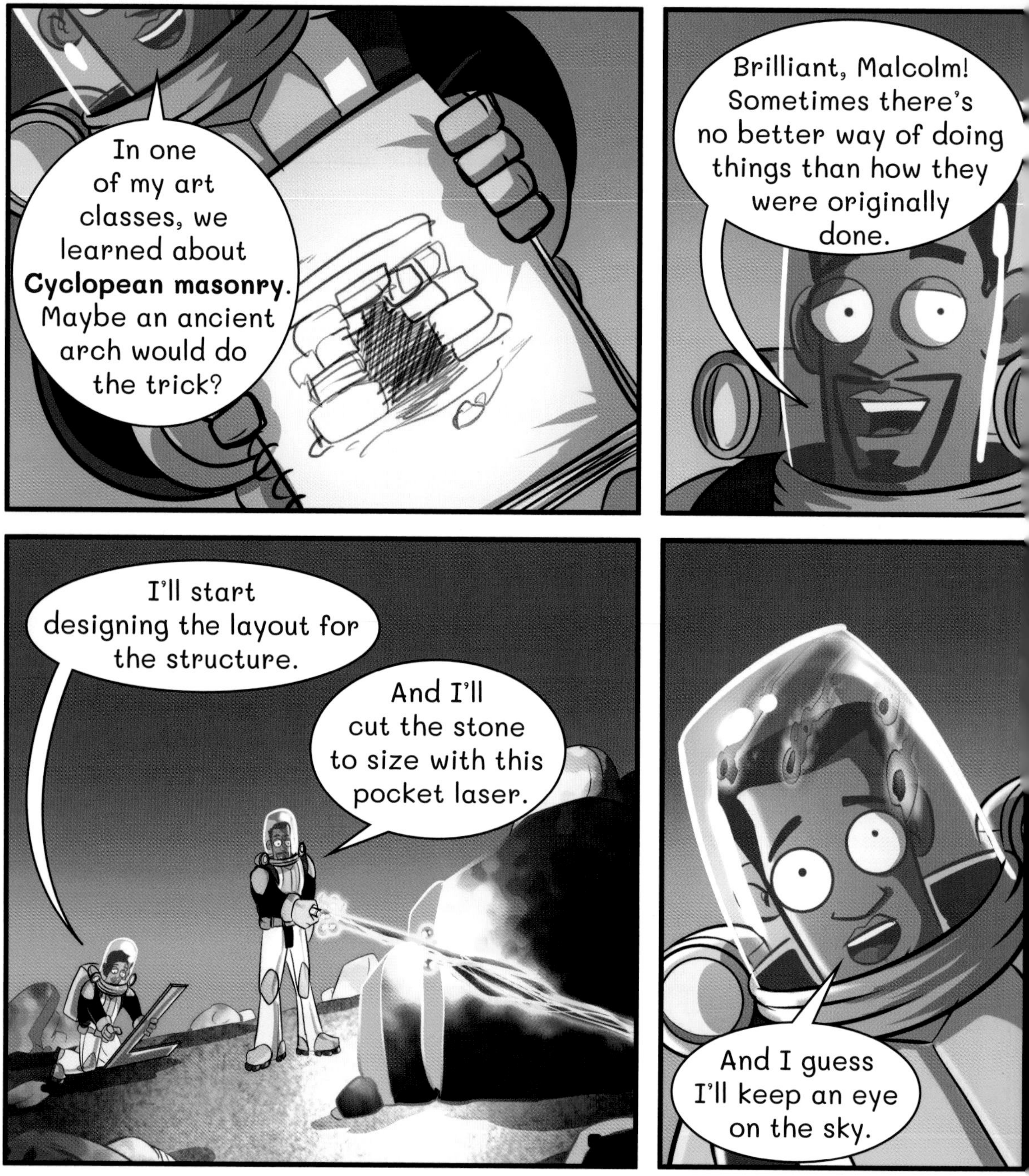
In one of my art classes, we learned about **Cyclopean masonry**. Maybe an ancient arch would do the trick?
Brilliant, Malcolm! Sometimes there's no better way of doing things than how they were originally done.
I'll start designing the layout for the structure.
And I'll cut the stone to size with this pocket laser.
And I guess I'll keep an eye on the sky.

SCIENCE FACT

Sometimes, meteors burn really bright. They ca be seen over a wide area. These meteors are called fireballs.

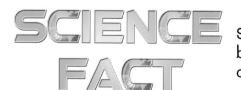

Cyclopean masonry: a type of stonework that uses huge boulders and no mortar to hold it together

THE FUNDAMENTALS OF ART

Let's put the FUN in the fundamentals of art by looking at how we can bring movement to a drawing. Look at these 2 images of the zebrax that Malcolm created with his pencil and imagination. Which one appears to be slithering and chewing?

•Start by drawing a line of action. A straight line implies fast and direct movement. A curved line suggests a flow and grace.

•From there, draw your character in the same direction or course as your line of action.

•When drawing your character, alternate between straight and curved lines. A character with only straight lines will look stiff and statue-like.

•Study the **anatomy** of what you are drawing. Understanding how it moves is key to creating natural movement on the page.

•Use expressions in your work. Characters come to life when they are showing their thoughts and emotions. You can show those in their facial features and body language.

ARTIST TIP: Another way to suggest movement is to add motion lines. These are lines that show how something is moving. If something is falling, you can add lines that show the path the object is taking. If a creature is chewing or eating, there may be lines around its cheeks or mouth.

anatomy: the study of a body, structure, or the way something works

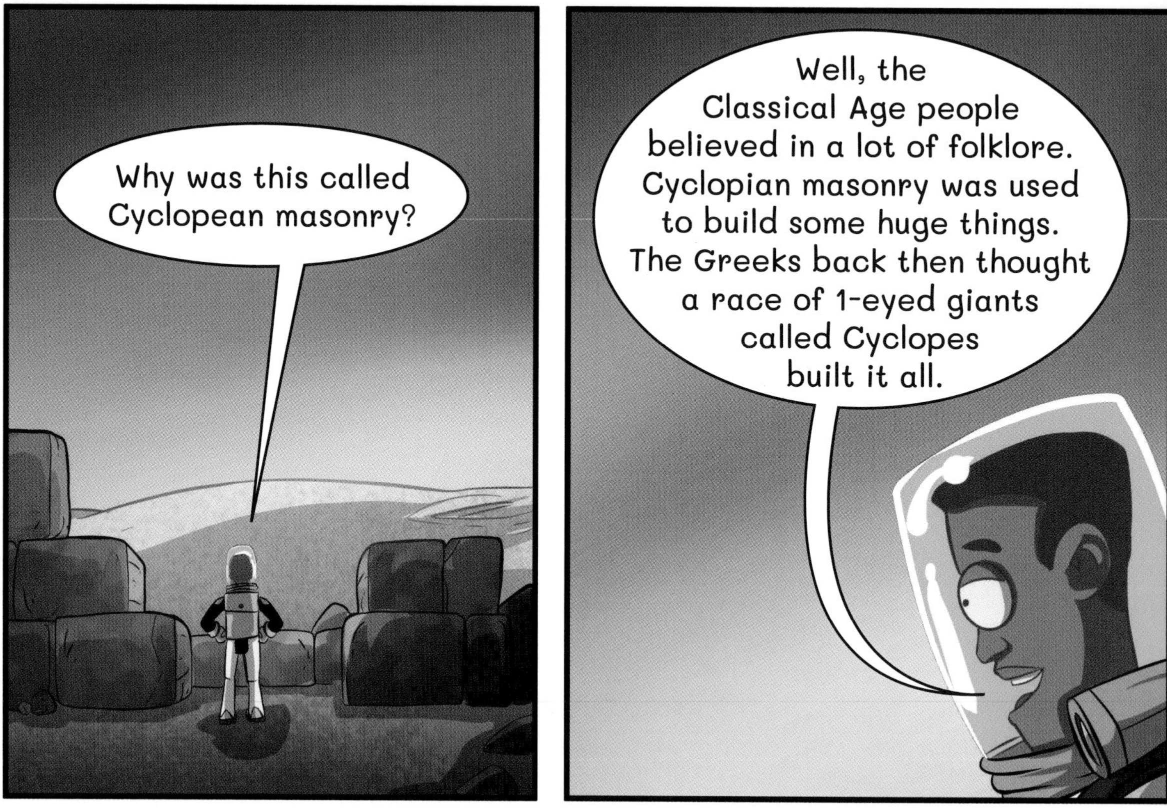
Why was this called Cyclopean masonry?
Well, the Classical Age people believed in a lot of folklore. Cyclopian masonry was used to build some huge things. The Greeks back then thought a race of 1-eyed giants called Cyclopes built it all.

SCIENCE FACT

The Classical Age of ancient Greece took place between about 500 and 323 BCE. Math and astronomy as we know it were developed during the classical age.

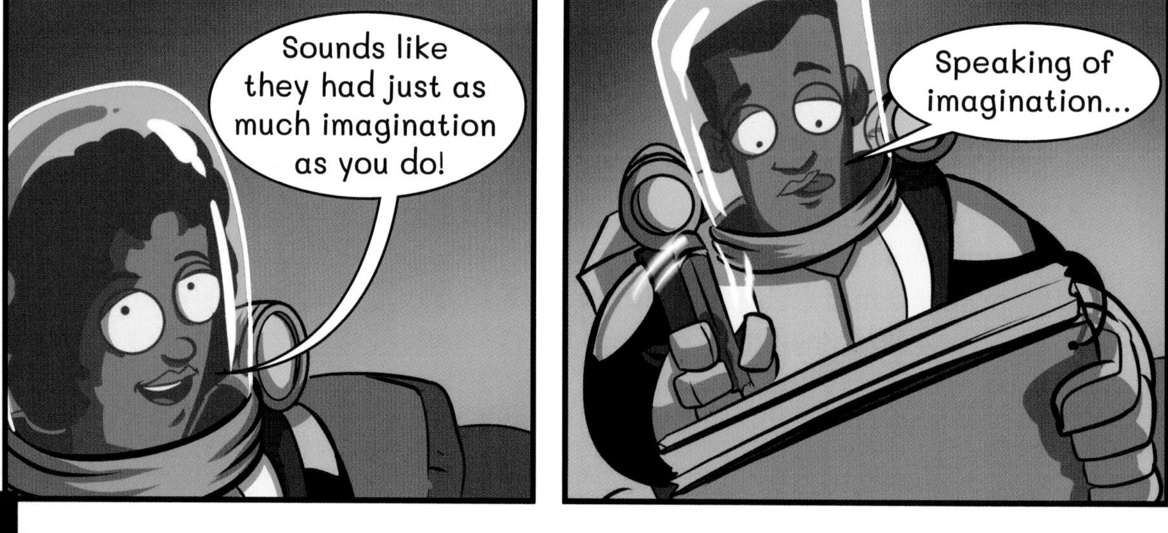
Sounds like they had just as much imagination as you do!
Speaking of imagination...

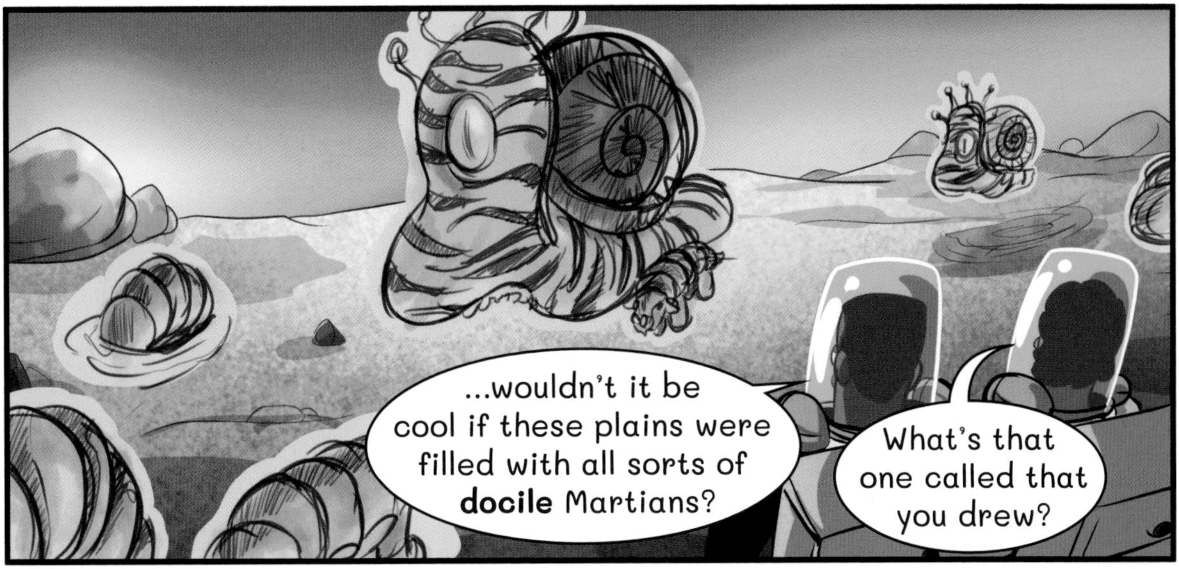
...wouldn't it be cool if these plains were filled with all sorts of **docile** Martians?
What's that one called that you drew?

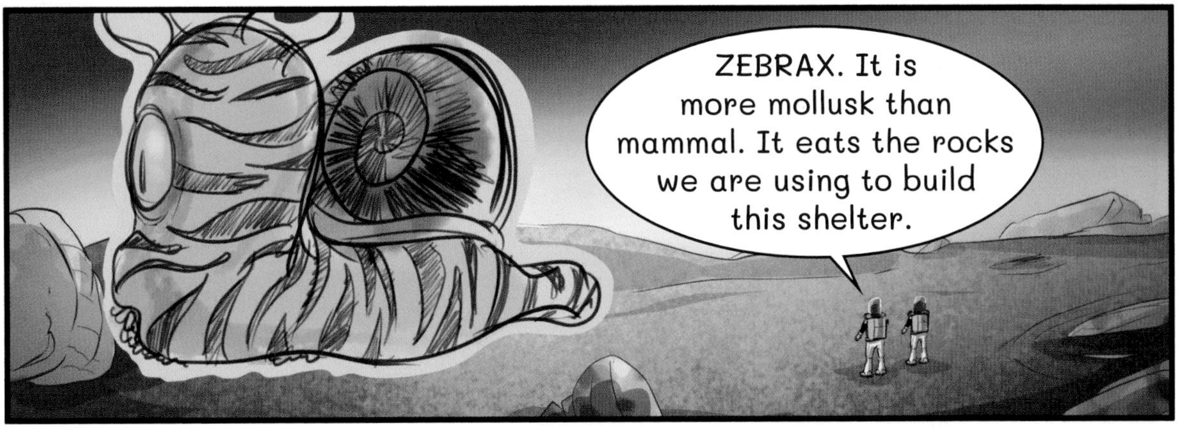
ZEBRAX. It is more mollusk than mammal. It eats the rocks we are using to build this shelter.

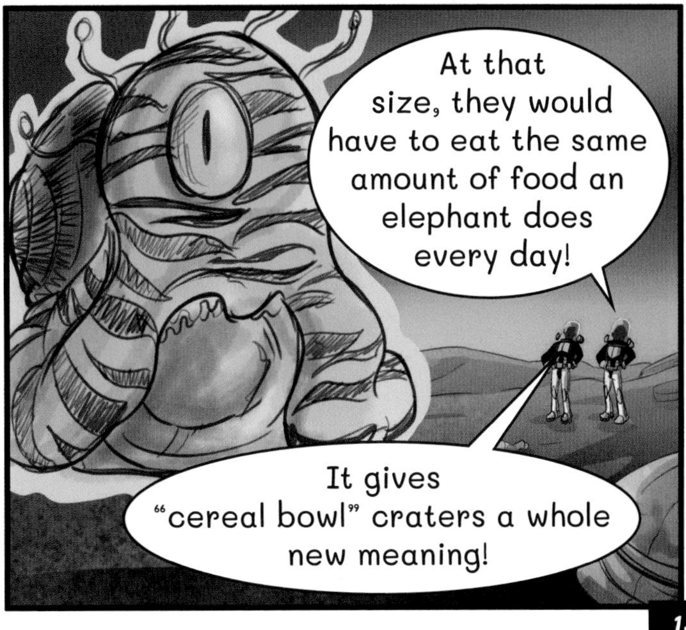
At that size, they would have to eat the same amount of food an elephant does every day!
It gives "cereal bowl" craters a whole new meaning!

SCIENCE FACT

Elephants eat 300 pounds (136 kilograms) of food every day. As impressive as that is, the blue whale eats up to 4 tons a day!

docile: not aggressive

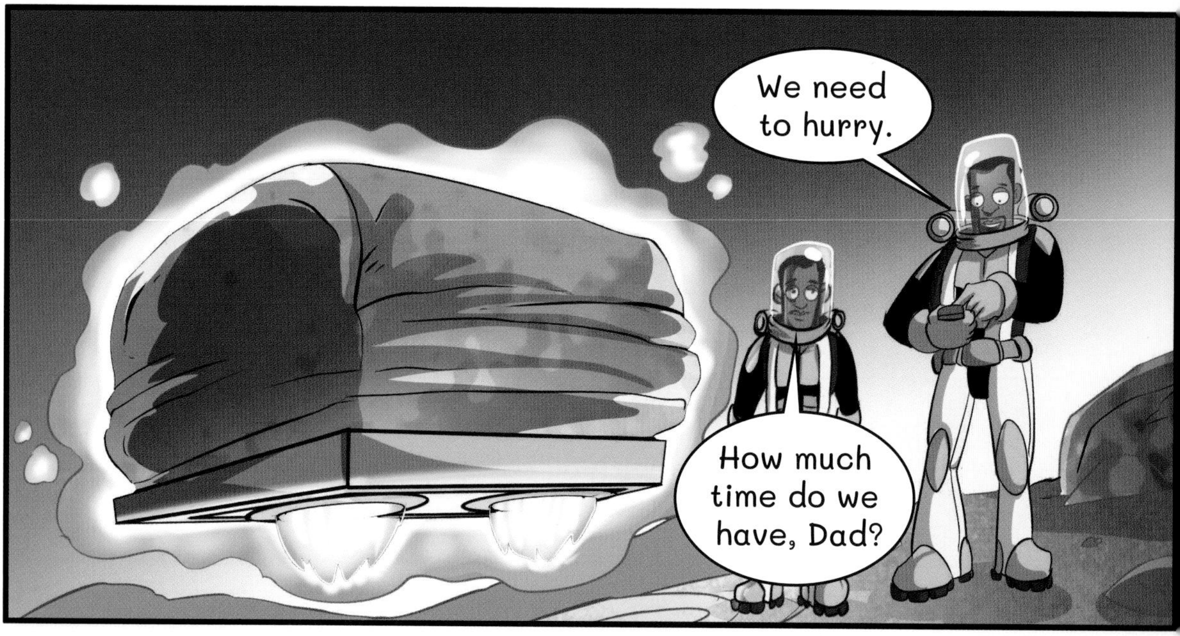
We need to hurry.
How much time do we have, Dad?

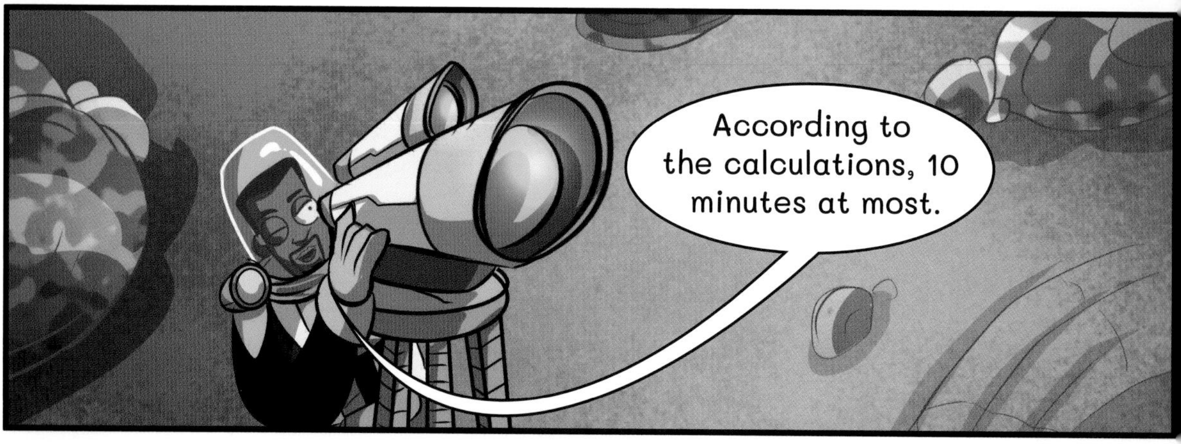
According to the calculations, 10 minutes at most.

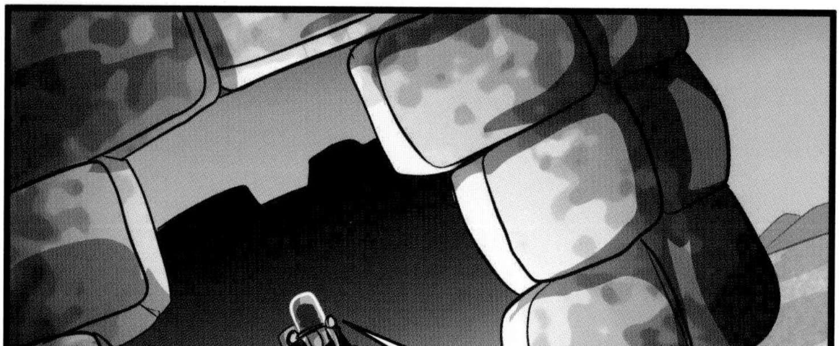
We only need 1 more stone to place on top of this arch. It has to be flat.

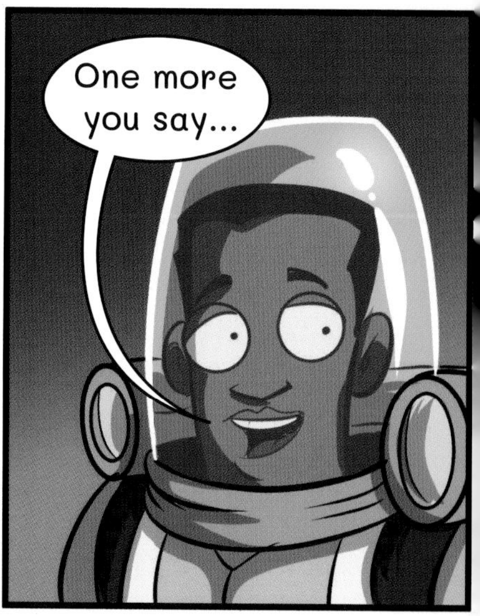
One more you say...

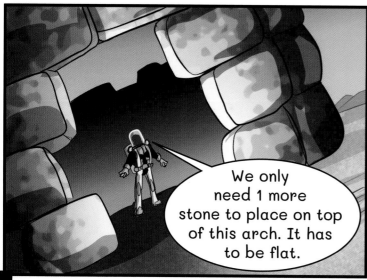

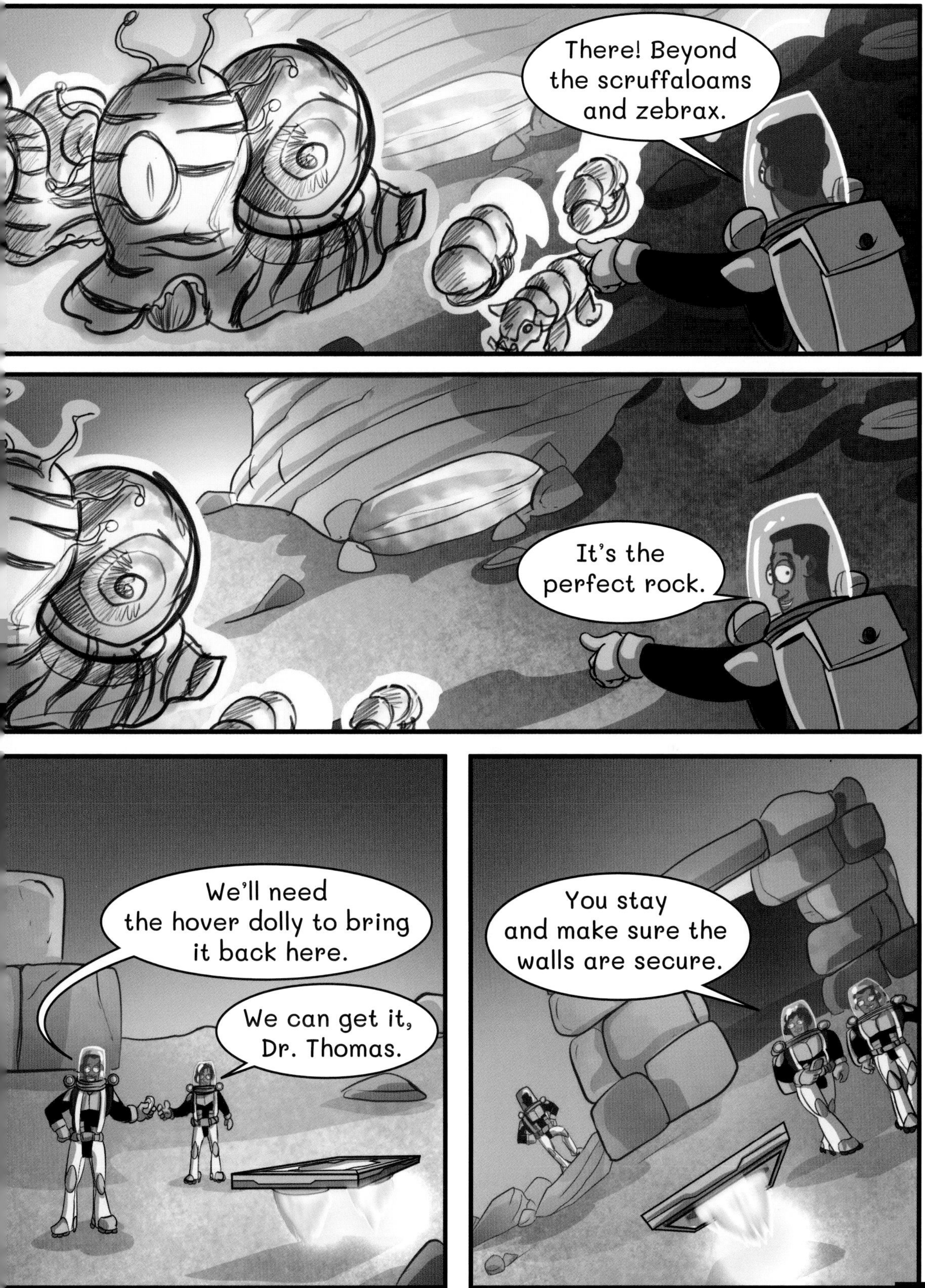
There! Beyond the scruffaloams and zebrax.
It's the perfect rock.
We'll need the hover dolly to bring it back here.
We can get it, Dr. Thomas.
You stay and make sure the walls are secure.

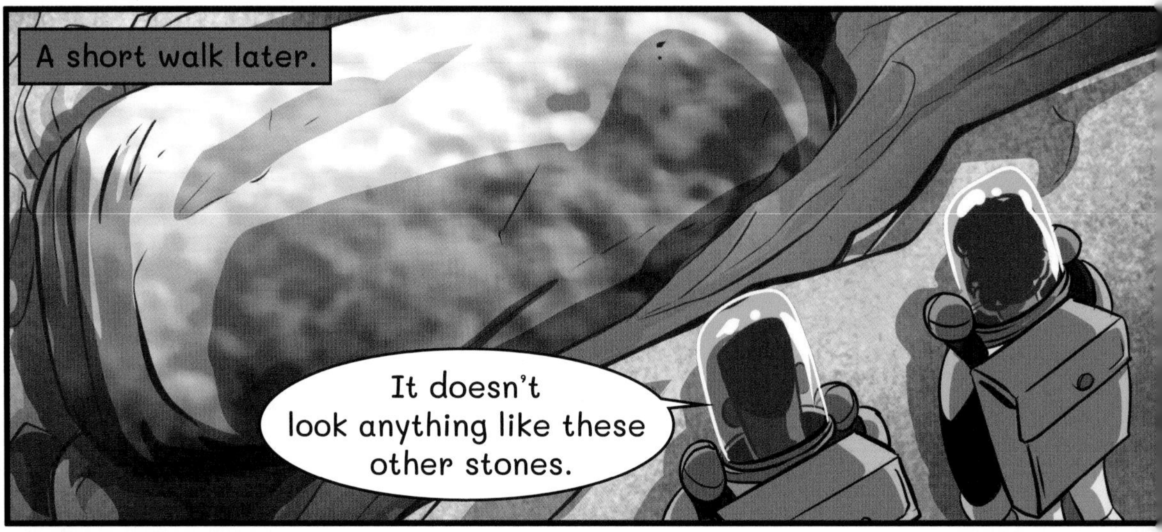
A short walk later.
It doesn't look anything like these other stones.

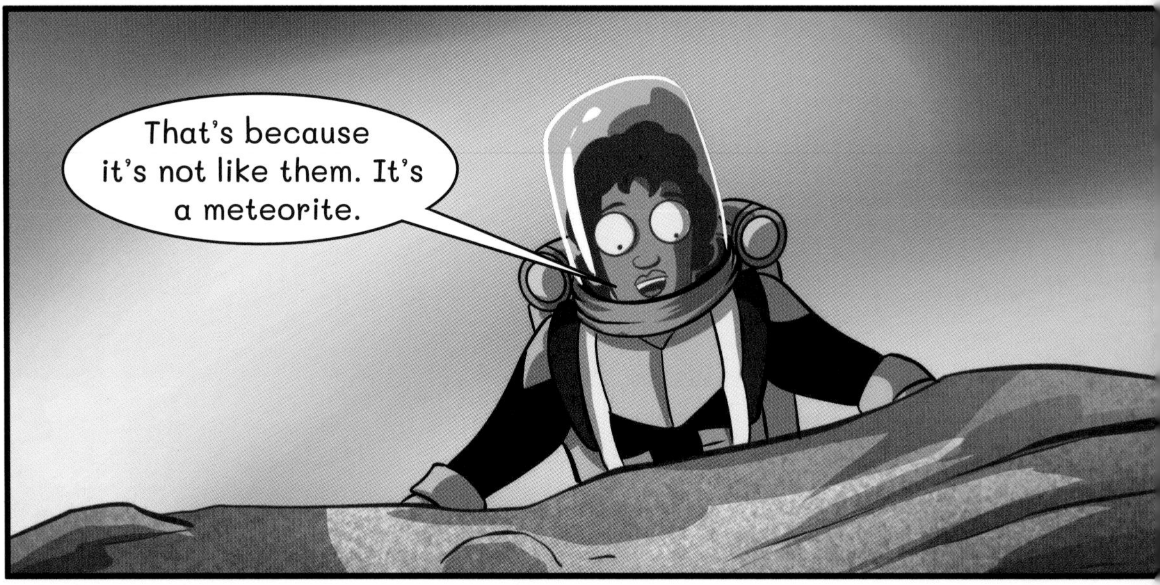
That's because it's not like them. It's a meteorite.

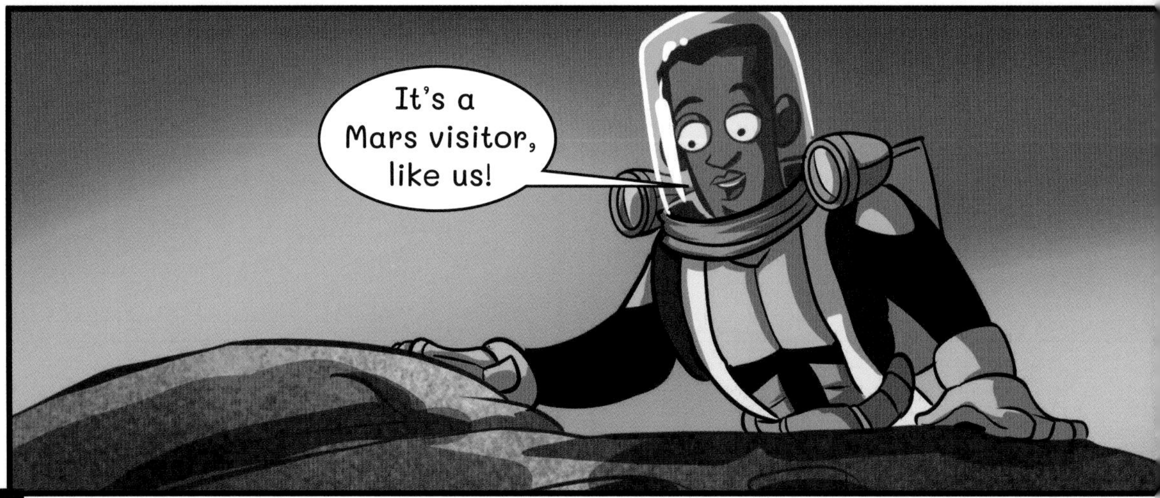
It's a Mars visitor, like us!

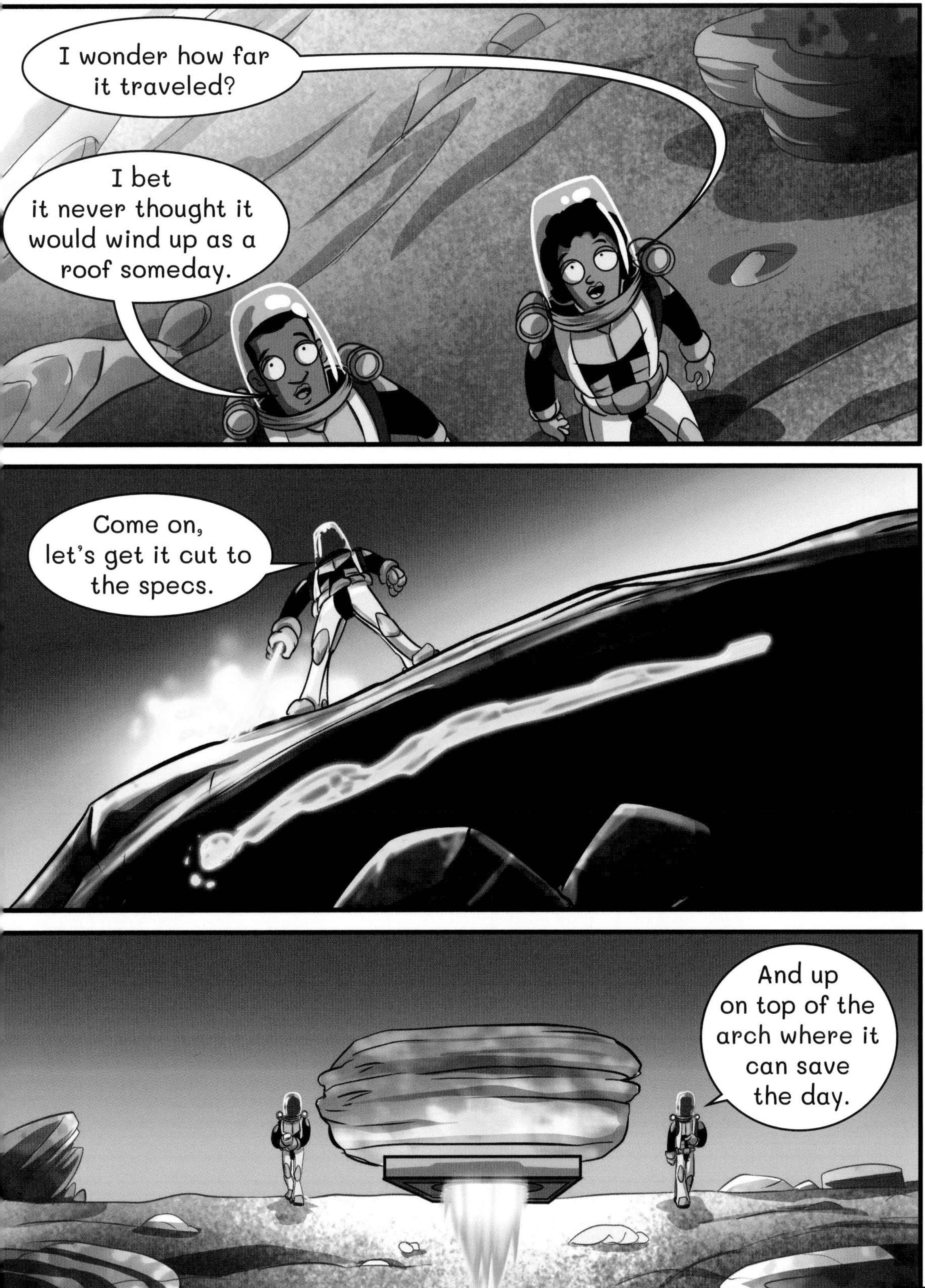
I wonder how far it traveled?
I bet it never thought it would wind up as a roof someday.
Come on, let's get it cut to the specs.
And up on top of the arch where it can save the day.

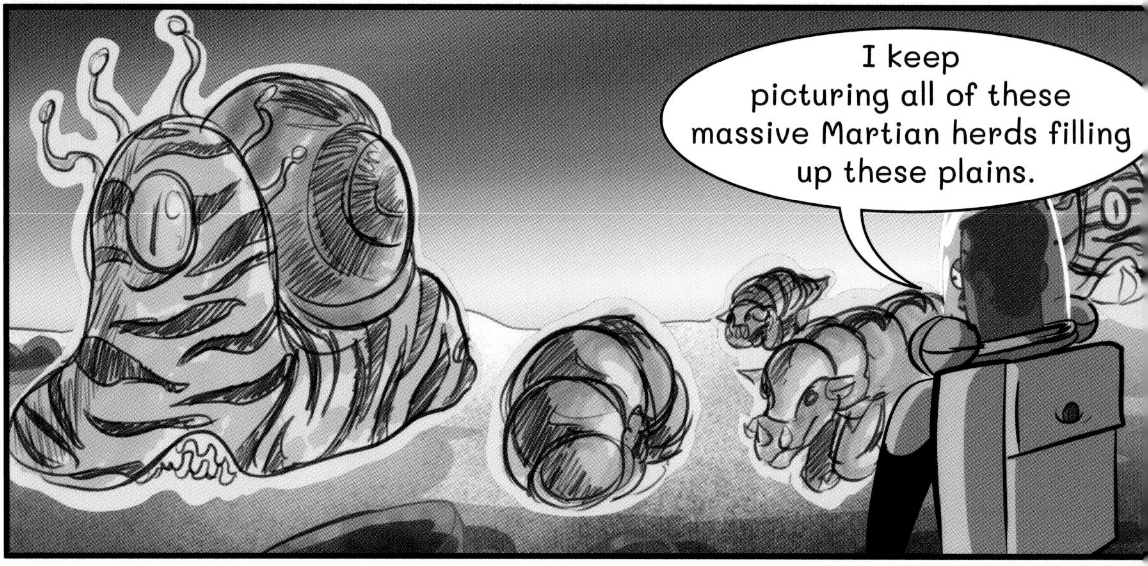
I keep picturing all of these massive Martian herds filling up these plains.

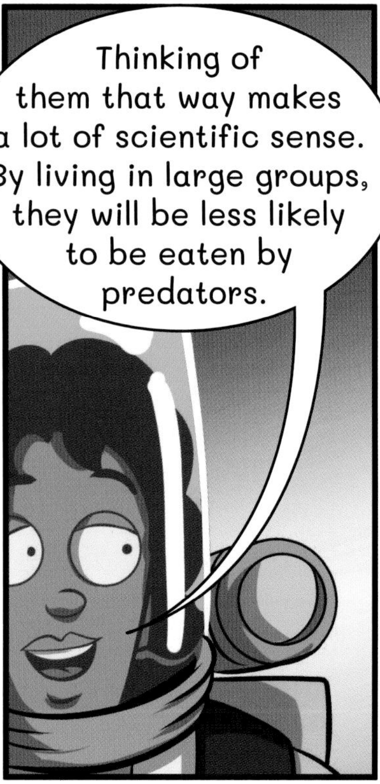
Thinking of them that way makes a lot of scientific sense. By living in large groups, they will be less likely to be eaten by predators.

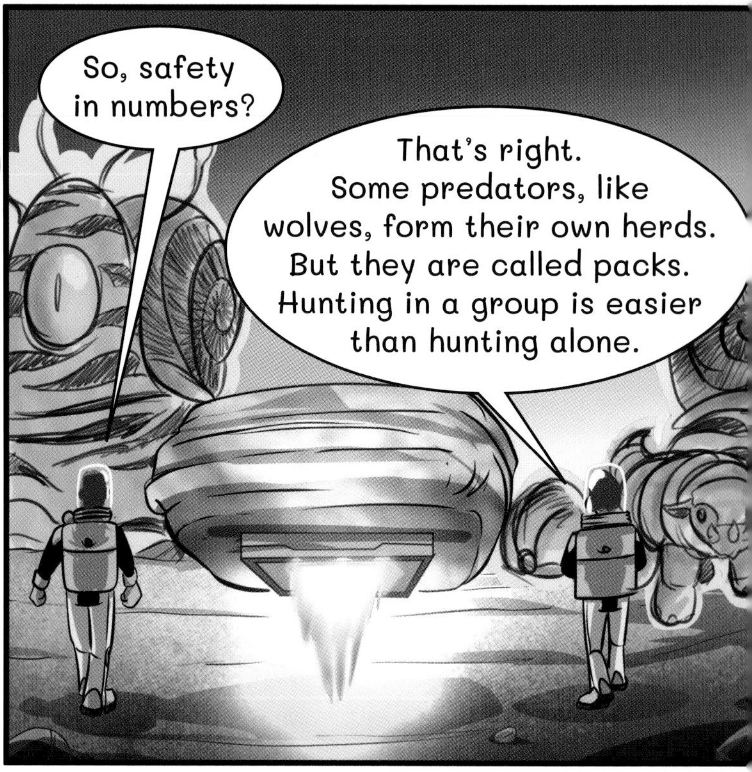
So, safety in numbers?
That's right. Some predators, like wolves, form their own herds. But they are called packs. Hunting in a group is easier than hunting alone.

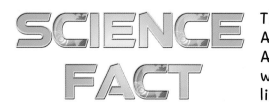

SCIENCE FACT

The Great Plains wolf is native to North America. They live in packs of 5 to 6 wolve Although once considered threatened, the were removed from the endangered speci list in 2007.

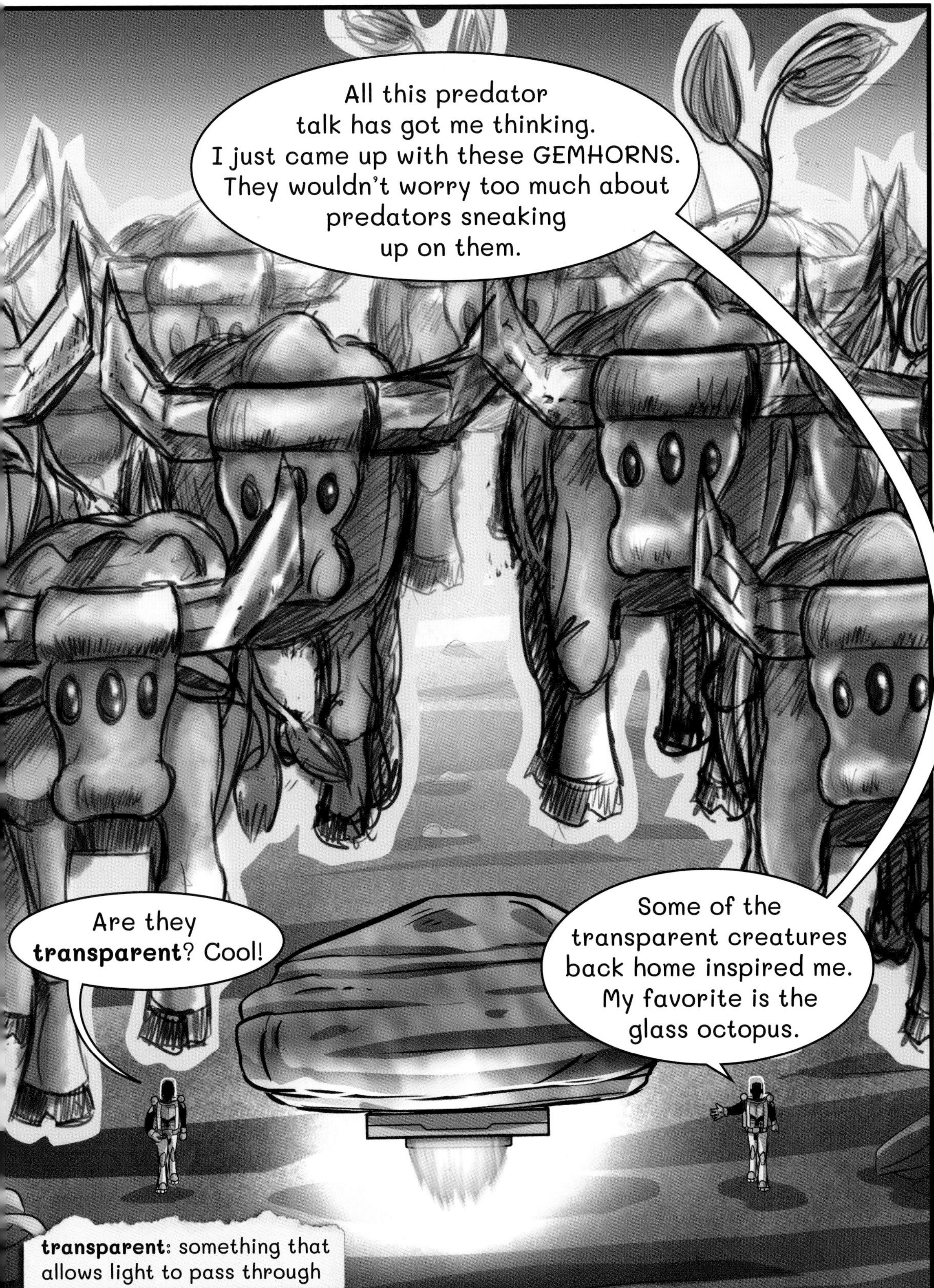
All this predator talk has got me thinking. I just came up with these GEMHORNS. They wouldn't worry too much about predators sneaking up on them.
Are they **transparent**? Cool!
Some of the transparent creatures back home inspired me. My favorite is the glass octopus.

transparent: something that allows light to pass through

Transparancy helps the rest of the gemhorns see what's going on outside of the herd.

Thank goodness you're back. We only have a few minutes before it starts raining down on us.

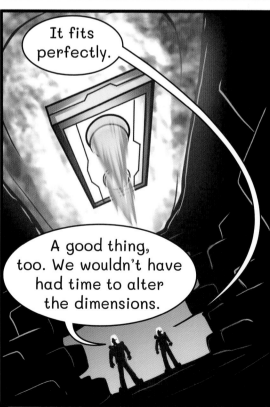

It fits perfectly.

A good thing, too. We wouldn't have had time to alter the dimensions.

Quickly, everyone. The meteor shower is here!

MARS SURVIVAL TIPS

The dinosaurs did not survive an asteroid or meteor shower on Earth. That does not mean the Martians of Mars would share the same fate! Here are some tips for surviving a meteor shower.

•It's important to understand that most meteorites are small. You would not even know that they were there unless you were near the impact site.

•Before they hit the ground, they are called meteors. Once they make contact with the atmosphere, they are called meteorites.

•Small meteors that enter the atmosphere burn up or break into smaller pieces before reaching the surface.

•Surprisingly, meteorites can cause more damage when they land in the ocean. Tsunamis can be deadly. For this reason, it is best to leave coastal areas and head to higher elevation.

•If meteorites are going to hit the planet's surface, go underground for safety. Seek shelter in a bunker or basement.

•The impact would cause harmful gases to escape into the atmosphere. This air would be dangerous to breathe. Gas masks should be worn for protection.

•These harmful gases would eventually create **acid rain**. Stay safe by staying in the shelter.

acid rain: precipitation that can cause harm to living things and the environment

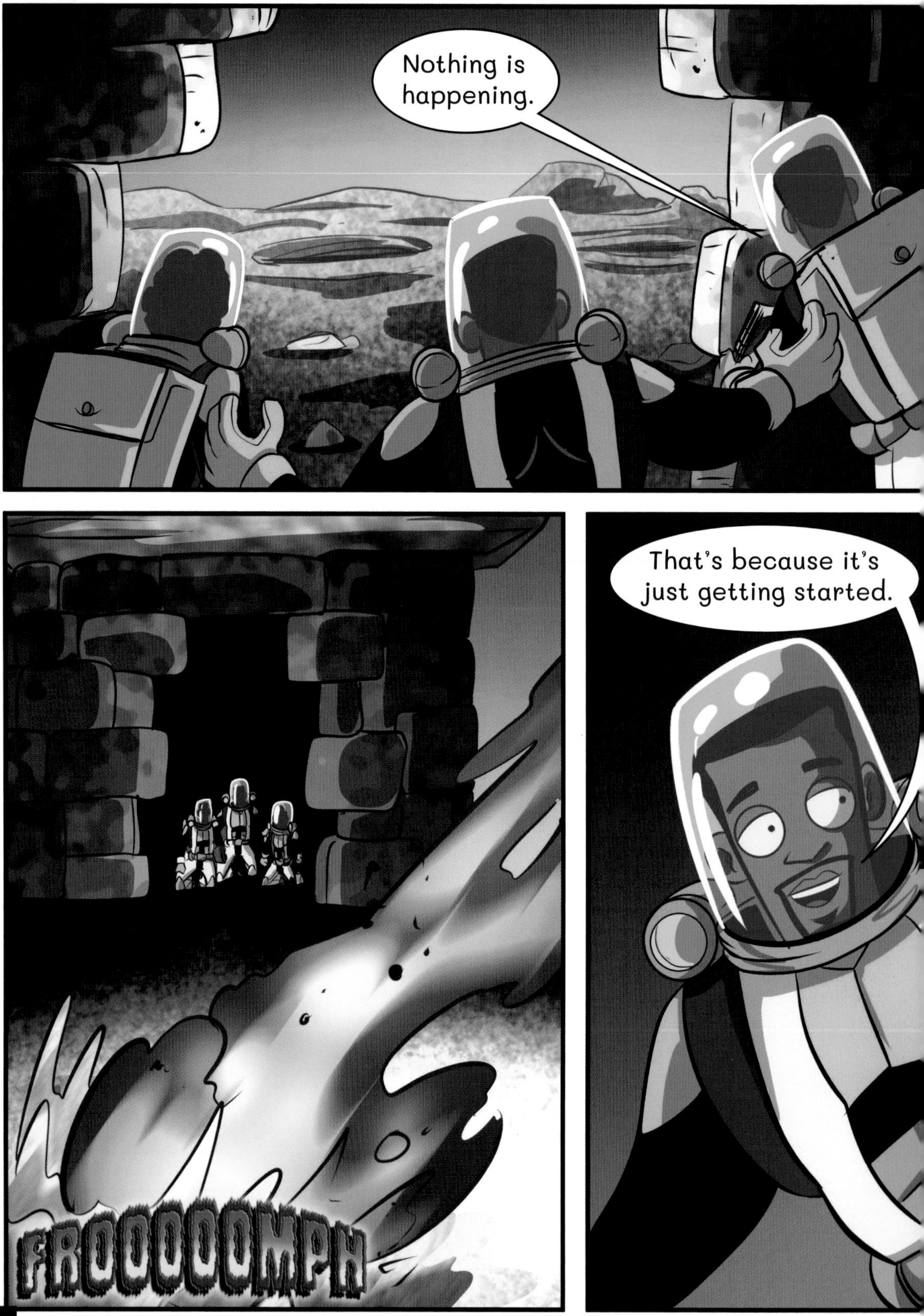
Nothing is happening.
FROOOOOOMPH
That's because it's just getting started.

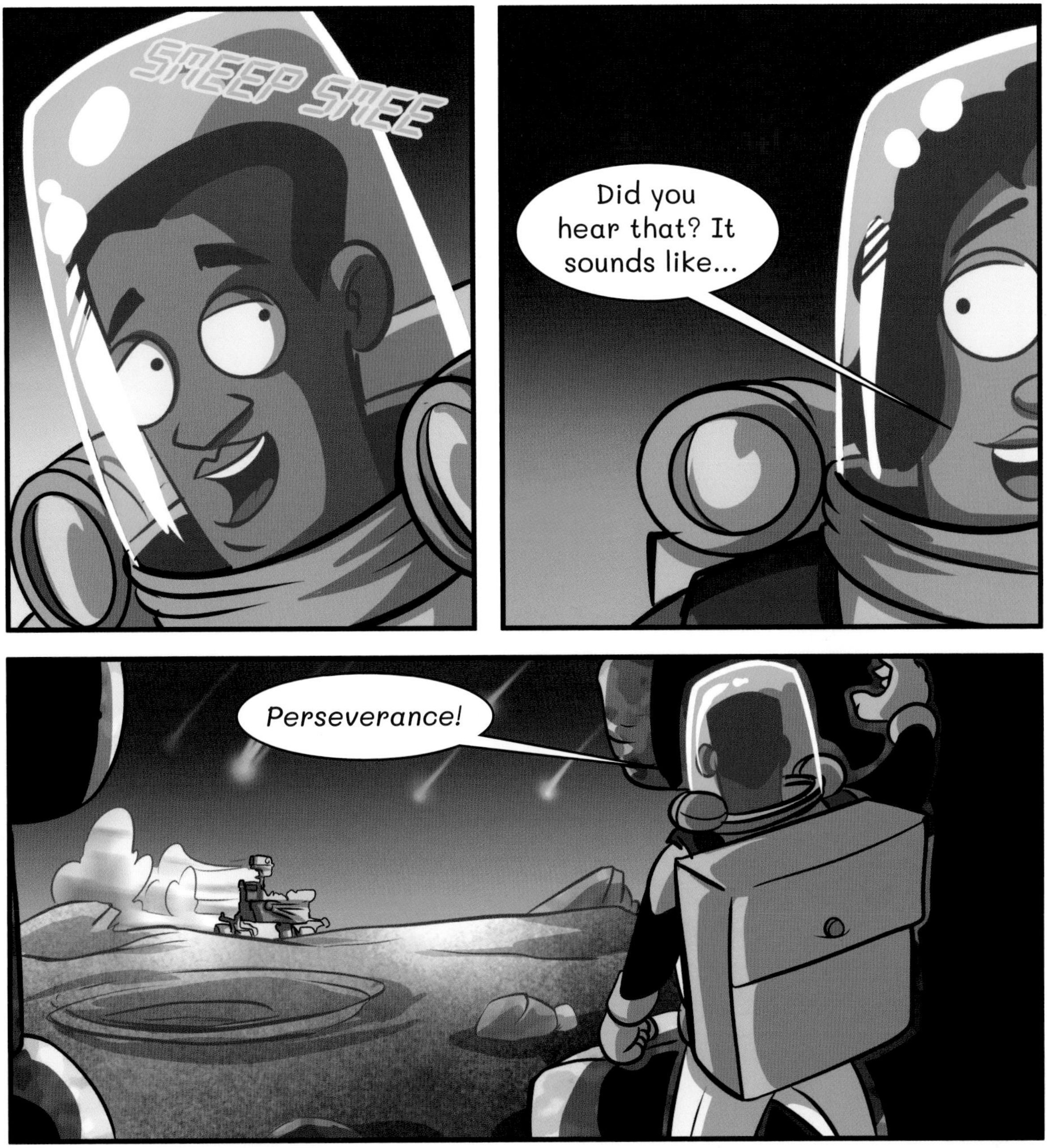
SMEEP SMEE
Did you hear that? It sounds like...
Perseverance!

MARS FACT

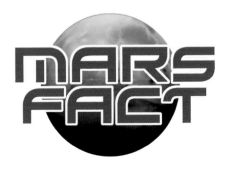

The rover *Perseverance* arrived on Mars February 18, 2021. It was built by engineers and scientists from NASA's Jet Propulsion Laboratory.

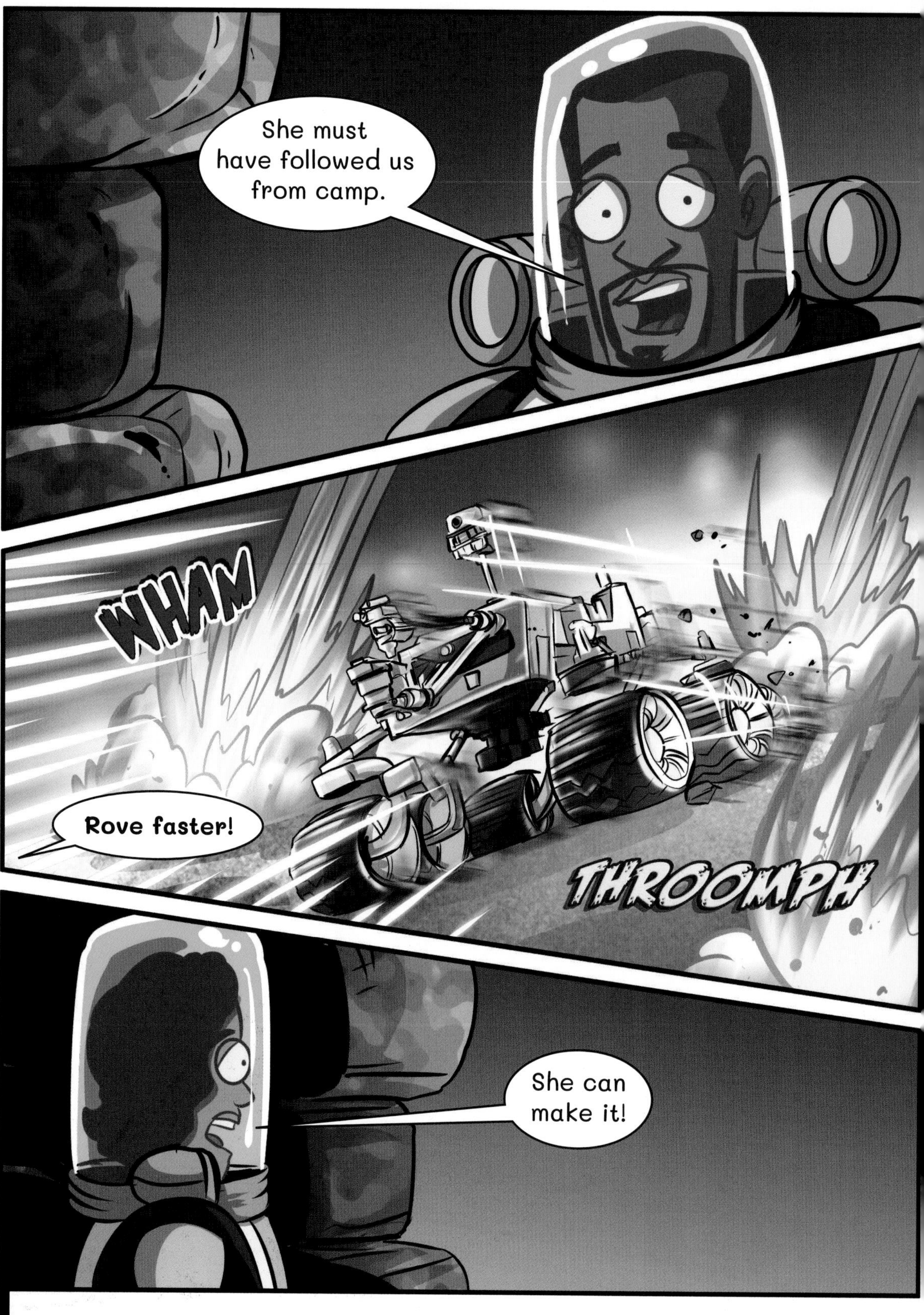
She must have followed us from camp.
WHAM
Rove faster!
THROOMPH
She can make it!

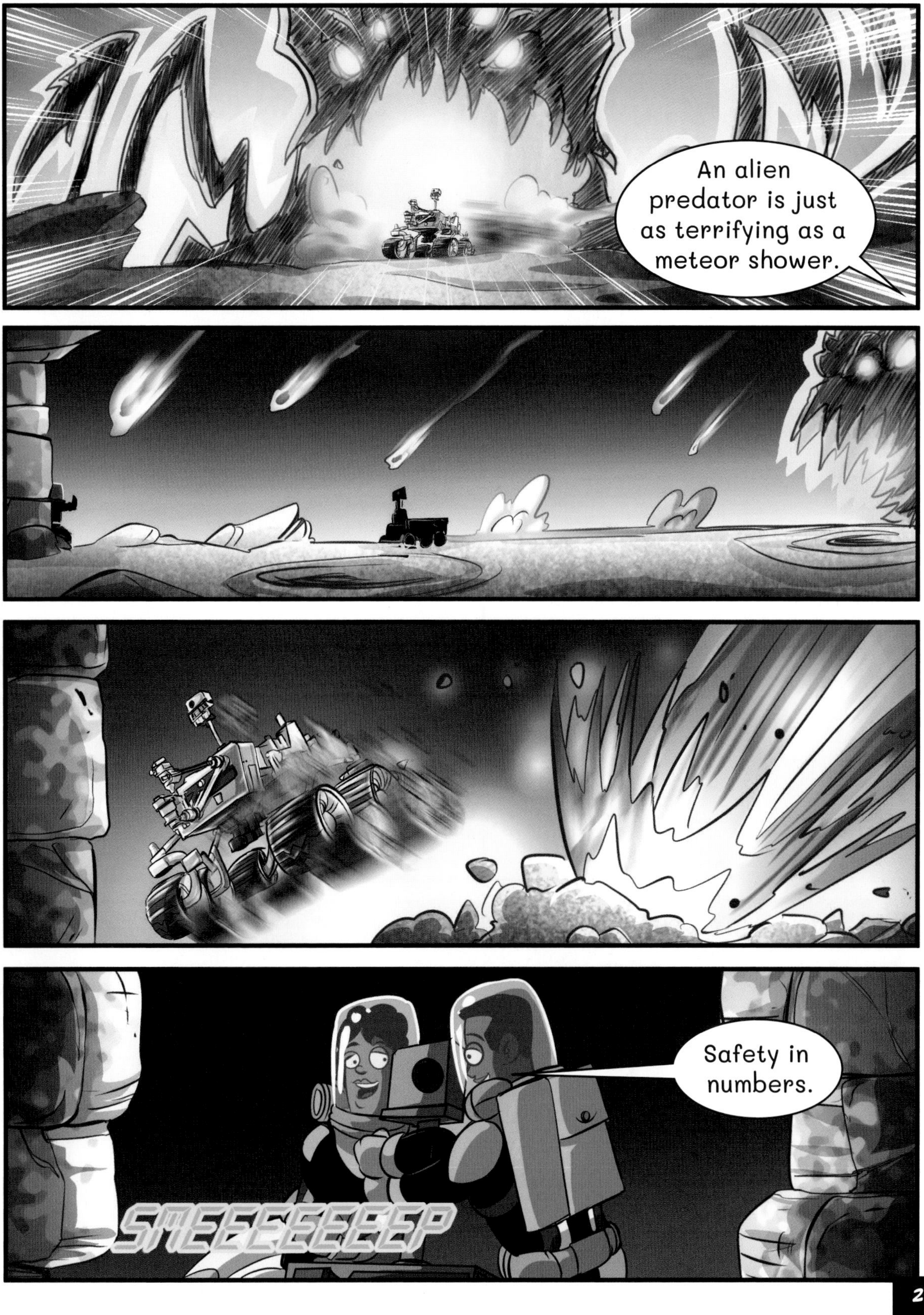
An alien predator is just as terrifying as a meteor shower.
Safety in numbers.
SMEEEEEEEP

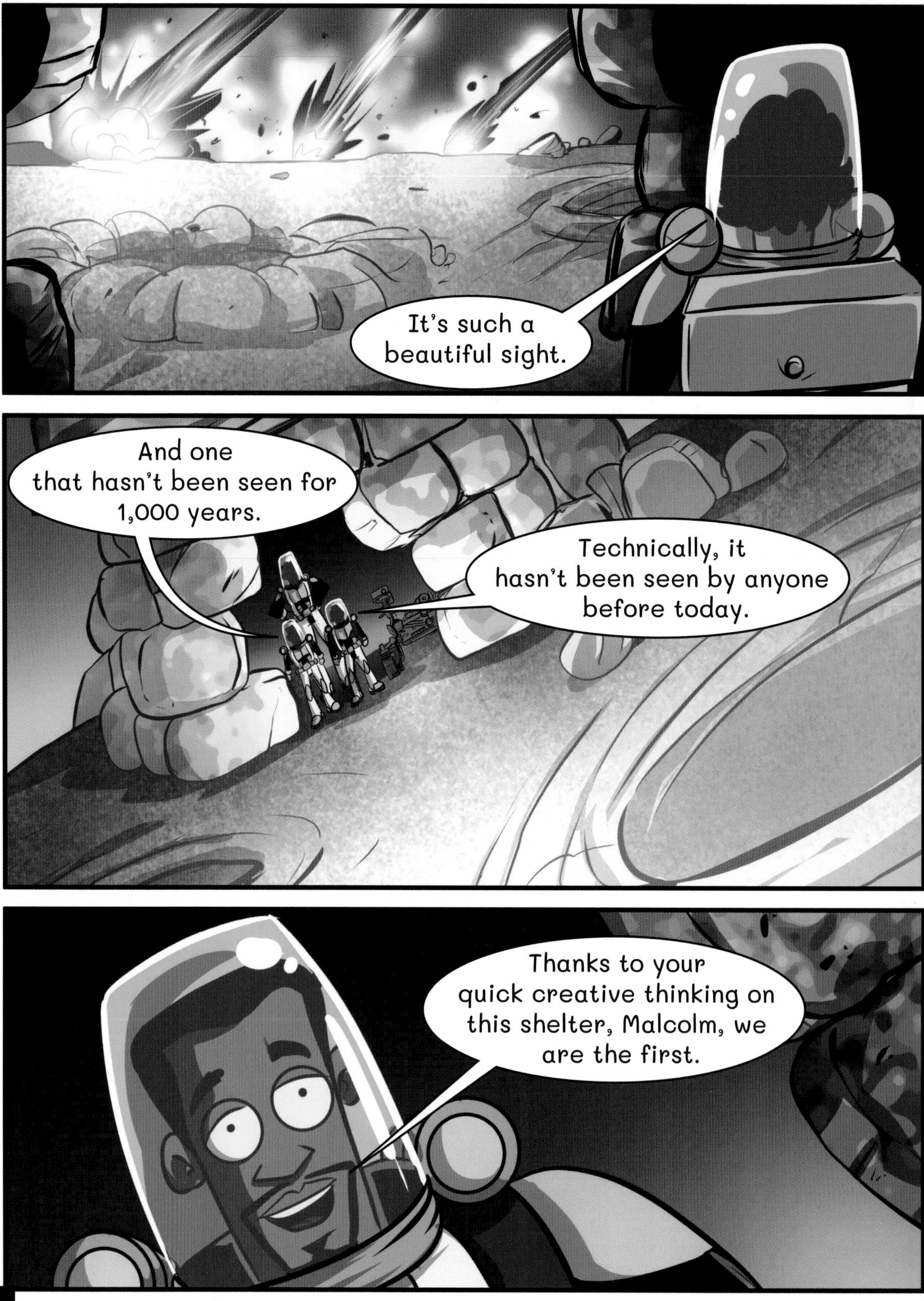
It's such a beautiful sight.
And one that hasn't been seen for 1,000 years.
Technically, it hasn't been seen by anyone before today.
Thanks to your quick creative thinking on this shelter, Malcolm, we are the first.

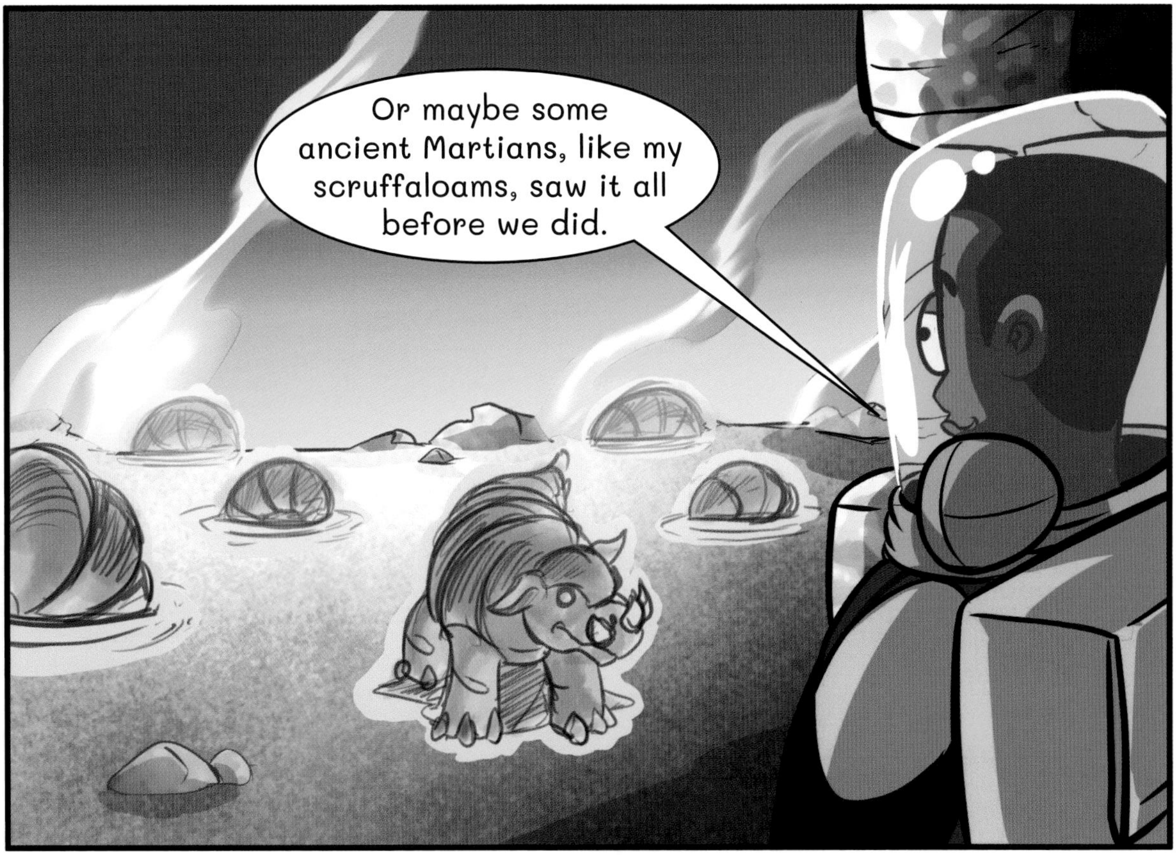
Or maybe some ancient Martians, like my scruffaloams, saw it all before we did.

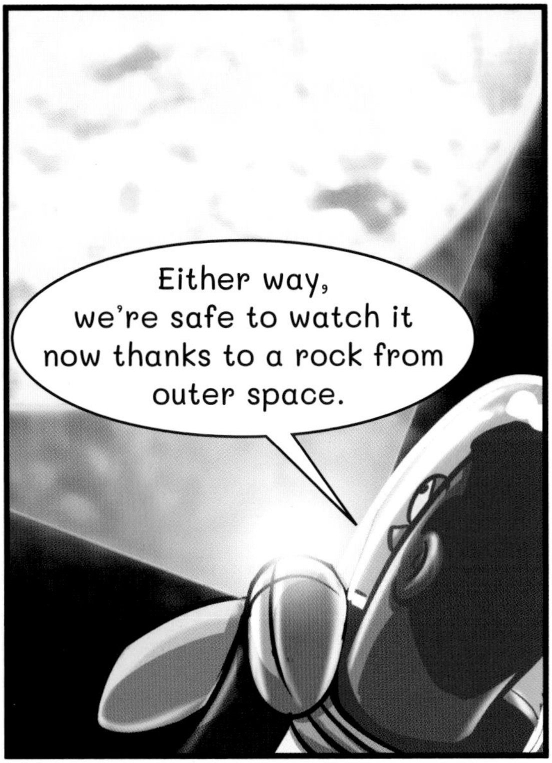
Either way, we're safe to watch it now thanks to a rock from outer space.

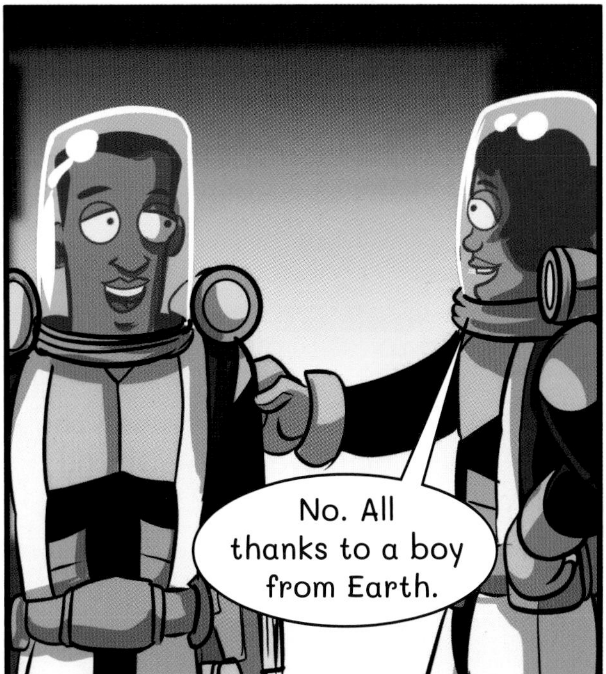
No. All thanks to a boy from Earth.

THE CRATER CREATOR

Mars is littered with impact craters. You can easily create a few of your own at home without the help of meteorites.

WHAT YOU NEED

- shallow pan
- white flour
- spoon
- cocoa powder
- marbles

STEPS TO TAKE

1. You may make a bit of a mess. Be sure to pick a place that is suitable for the experiment.

2. Fill the bottom of the pan with about 1 inch (2.54 cm) of flour.

3. Use the spoon to sprinkle the cocoa powder over the surface of the flour. Put just enough so that the flour is not fully visible.

4. Hold the marbles over the pan. Then drop them into the flour. They will crash down into the surface like miniature meteorites. Don't be afraid to add your own sound effects!

5. What do you notice when the marbles hit the surface? When happens to the flour layer beneath the powdered chocolate? Does some of it come to the surface?

6. Remember, no 2 meteorites are the same shape and size. Try the experiment with a few other items around your house and see if they make bigger—or smaller—craters.

LEARN MORE

BOOKS

Downs, Mike. *Imagining Space*. Vero Beach, FL: Roarke Educational Media, 2021.

Huddleston, Emma. *Explore the Planets*. Minneapolis, MN: ABDO Publishing, a division of ABDO, 2021.

WEBSITES

Curious Kids: Can People Colonize Mars?
https://theconversation.com/curious-kids-can-people-colonize-mars-122251

Kids ask, experts answer: Can we colonize Mars?

NASA: Perseverance
https://www.nasa.gov/perseverance

Learn about Perseverance's mission to Mars and get all the latest news and discoveries.

THE MARTIANS

SCRUFFALOAMS

Malcolm imagines these armadillo-like Martians to take shelter inside of their own shells during the meteor showers that rain down on the plains.

GEMHORNS

Outfitted with quartz horns, Malcolm draws these goat-like Martians to be transparent. This helps them look out for predators while traveling in large packs.

ZEBRAX

Malcolm thought up these gigantic slug-like Martians to eat the many different kinds of rocks that litter the Mars plains.

GLOSSARY

acid rain (A-sud rein) precipitation that can cause harm to living things and the environment

anatomy (uh-NA-tuh-mee) the study of a body, structure or the way something works

artificial intelligence (aar-tuh-FI-shul in-TEH-luh-jns) machines that perform tasks requiring human intelligence

automated (AA-tuh-mei-tuhd) the use of automatic equipment, such as machines

comet (KAA-muht) frozen chunks of dust, rock and ice that release gas and heat up as they travel close to the sun

craters (KRAY-terz) circular depressions in the ground

Cyclopean masonry (SAI-klo-pee-an MEI-suhn-ree) a type of stonework that uses huge boulders and no mortar to hold it together

meteorites (MEE-tee-ur-aits) pieces of a comet or asteroid that reach the surface of a planet

mollusk (MAA-luhsk) an invertebrate animal, such as snails, mussels, and slugs; mollusks have soft bodies and many have hard shells

orbits (OR-buhts) curved paths of an object around a star, planet, or moon

survey (ser-VAY) to examine and record the features of an area

transparent (tranz-PEH-ruhnt) light can pass through so you can see to the other side

INDEX